IN THE ORCHARD,
THE SWALLOWS

Peter Hobbs

IN THE ORCHARD, THE SWALLOWS

Europa
editions

Europa Editions
214 West 29th Street
New York, N.Y. 10001
www.europaeditions.com
info@europaeditions.com

Library of Congress Cataloging in Publication Data is available
ISBN 978-1-60945-183-7

Hobbs, Peter
In the Orchard, the Swallows

Book design by Emanuele Ragnisco
www.mekkanografici.com

Cover illustration © jameslee1/iStock

Prepress by Grafica Punto Print – Rome

Printed in the USA

'Say: I seek refuge in the Lord of Daybreak'
—QURAN 113:1

IN THE ORCHARD,
THE SWALLOWS

THE ORCHARD

It is cold, despite the woollen shawl I have borrowed from Abbas. Beneath its weight my flesh is too sparse, the skin stretched tightly over bones. I have been climbing for a long time—it was dark when I left—but I cannot walk quickly enough to get the heat to rise in my blood. My shivering grows violent and my teeth rattle uncontrollably, the sound echoing in my head. The cold causes my neck to ache and my jaw to stiffen.

The air, though, is blissful and clear. It brings the ragged mountains close, chisels their details finely to my eye. The peaks are yellow in the early sun. Later, the sunlight will climb down from the mountains and descend this road into the valley below, restoring the colours that were lost to the pale washed night.

This walk exhausts me still. I am close to staggering when I arrive, my legs almost gone beneath me. After all the years away they have not readjusted to the mountains, and I can feel every step of the climb still in them. My breath comes heavily.

In the rose dawn light I greet the trees. Trace with my eyes their untidy forms. I imagined them for so long, summoning them up in the darkness when they were lost to me, and each morning now it is an acute pleasure to return to them. They are in blossom, their branches arrayed in scarlet and white.

To one side, as I circle the orchard, is the corn field. The crop has begun to emerge from the earth, ragged lines of green forming against the dark soil. I wonder if it will grow as tall as I remember it. I move around the furthest edge of the trees, following the low stone border until I reach its end, beside the largest tree. Here, I will wait. I press my palm against its bark, then turn to rest my back against it as I ease to the ground. My sandals slide forwards, and the feel of the cold dust on my feet is extraordinary; it runs as smoothly as water over my skin. Among the folds of my shawl I find the paper bag I have brought, and I take some of yesterday's bread from it, nibbling slowly at its edge.

The birds have woken and there are swallows in the orchard, carving arcing paths between the trees. Below them a fine layer of mist clings to the ground. Pomegranates are hardy plants, and the trees are showing little damage from the winter frosts, though they are growing wild and have not been pruned for some time, or else the pruning has been done inexpertly. The trees are growing old, and the orchard has not been renewed as it should; no new cuttings have been taken and planted. Still, they grow vigorously. Sprouting roots have been left unchecked, blurring what were once carefully trained trees into the wild bushes they long to be. The fruit will suffer for it. If I had the tools I would be tempted to tend to them, but they are no longer my own trees to tend. It is better that I do not touch them.

From where I sit I am able to look down over the valley. Can follow the thread of the road, cutting down the mountainside along its dusty ridge. At its far end, not yet visible in the light, is the town, your old home. There, at least, the market will still be waking into life. Here, all is peaceful.

I gather my breath. I try to imagine the weakness in my legs bleeding out into the dirt, being replaced by some vitality which ekes from the tree into my back. I wait as long as I am able, until the sun has found the road above and the skyline begins to glow bright, the mountain-tops white and blinding. The light will reach me soon. But I cannot stay to see it. In a few moments, before the evidence of life begins to show in the small house through the trees, before the farmer comes to his orchard and finds me here, I will stand and brush the sand from my shalwar, stretch once again to ease the aches in my muscles and joints, and begin the slow journey home.

ABBAS

I see I have written *home*, though the home I am staying in is not my own. It belongs to a man named Abbas. I am not sure how to describe him for you. He is not family, and yet I cannot call him my landlord, because I do not pay him any rent. If I said that he was my saviour, it would not be an exaggeration, but I will come to that story in time, and so for the moment I will simply say that he is my host.

His house is larger than the one I grew up in. It sits on the edge of a small village, some distance north and west of town, a few miles from the orchard. From the road it looks small, the simple sandy wall suggesting nothing more than a farmer's cottage. But the impression is deceptive, and the building is more extensive than it appears. Inside there are bedrooms for both Abbas and his daughter, Alifa. She is ten, the same age my youngest sister was when I last saw her, though it is clear I am some way yet from earning the right to be treated as a brother. I am patient in my efforts. There is a kitchen, and then beside that another small room which seems once to have been a larder, but which has been given over to me, a bed brought in and placed against the cool mud of the wall. And there is a study, its walls lined with books, its floor thick with overlapping carpets. Abbas spends much of the days there, when he is home, reading or writing. The house is filled with plants. Everywhere there are flashes of green. I can taste them in the air. The carpets and furniture throughout are simple, but clearly of a finer quality than I am accustomed to.

Behind the home is a walled garden, with a small terrace. There is a table, and two chairs, and beside them a tall electric fan, its green paint half given over to rust. I have not seen it in use, and do not think it has been working for some time, but it looks at home nonetheless, as though it has been forgotten, and in the process has gradually achieved the status of somehow belonging there, becoming its own ornament. But the garden, too, I will tell you about in time.

I remember waking here on my first day, lying on a charpoy, feeling the rough cords of the bed beneath my back softened by sheets. A doctor stood at my bedside. I did not know where I was. The walls of the strange larder seemed to slant in above me, though I realised later that it was just my dizziness. I felt a terrible weakness in my body, a buzzing in my arms and legs as though they were filled with insects. I was dressed in a shalwar kameez several sizes too large—though when Abbas tells the story, he has it that it was I who was several sizes too small.

He must have paid for the doctor to come, though he will not speak of the cost, when I ask him. The doctor listened briefly to my story and asked about my symptoms. I was so dehydrated I could hardly speak. When they tried to give me water my body would not keep it down. He left for me two plastic bottles of an oily, salted liquid to drink when I could. And he gave me pills, antibiotics, sour lozenges the size and shape of almonds. Even as it knew how much I needed them, my body tried to reject them, as it purged almost everything from it in those days. I wonder if there was something in me that did not want to return from illness. Something that preferred to remain latched closely to it, resigned to circle down into the darkness, to be consumed.

Before he left the doctor massaged my limbs, a tight circled grip travelling along them.

'It will help the circulation,' he said.

His hands fitted completely around my thin arms, my emaciated legs.

When he had gone Abbas came into the room, and I tried to stand, respectful before my elder, but I was not able to, and collapsed into darkness. That is all I remember of my first day here. I woke once more, and from the coolness knew that it was night. I drank some water, and finally kept down the doctor's pills, and then I slept. I slept for days, lost to monstrous, appalling dreams.

So I did not meet my host for a long time, and it was a full week before the fever subsided and my head cleared enough to properly speak with him. He came in through the door as I was trying to get out of bed, though my head and limbs swam with sickness. He must have heard me moving. He introduced himself, and I gave him my name.

'You mentioned many names in your sleep,' he said, with a smile. 'And not one of them your own.'

I wondered what I had said, of whom I had spoken. Did I say your name? I have kept it secret for so long. I tried to remember, but I knew nothing of the night that had gone. I tried again to rise.

'No,' he said. 'You must lie back. Rest a while. Here, there is water beside you.'

He approached, but saw me flinch in response, and stepped back. The instinct is not easily lost. Abbas must have seen that I did not trust him, and I wonder what he read in it then. Perhaps only confusion.

'I want to thank you,' I said, after I had taken some water. 'For your hospitality. But I have to go.'

'You are not at all well enough,' he said.

'I cannot stay,' I said, and flinched again as he came closer, but I was too weak to protest, and I allowed him to ease my shoulders against the bed once more. I have learned in the hardest manner possible to read the intentions of others, and I understood, finally, that he did not mean me harm.

'Of course you must,' he said. 'You will stay until you are stronger. You need far more rest than you have had. I cannot let you leave in such a state.'

And so I did not leave, and in the end I have stayed with him a long time. How fortunate I am to have found him! Or, it would be truer to say, how fortunate I was to have been found by him. I will not forget my good fortune, and I will repay him for his expenses, for the medical bills, as I will repay all of his kindnesses to me, as soon as I am able.

HOMECOMING

The first time I came here it was not to visit the orchard, merely to return to what I thought was my home. I came one afternoon early in the year, perhaps three weeks after that first day with Abbas. He did not think me well enough to travel, but I was impatient to see my family, and I came as soon as I was able to walk. I did not walk the whole distance. Abbas helped me along as far as the end of the village, and we waited there for a car to come by. He flagged it down, and spoke for a moment to the driver, whom he seemed to know, then waved me over and opened the door for me. He sought reassurance several times that I knew where I was going, but of course I knew the way. He made me promise to return if I did not find what I was looking for. Before I left, he handed me a bottle of water for the journey.

The car took me most of the way up the hill, and when the driver indicated that this was as far as he was going, I stepped out, and walked the last stretch myself. I knew as soon as I arrived that my family was gone. There was the state of the orchard, for one thing: my father would not have allowed it to decline in this way. But I did not see that until later. No, it was something else, some change in the air as I approached. How do I explain it? There were few outward changes to the house, and yet the place had a feeling of unfamiliarity to it. I felt a small stone of panic in my stomach. I thought for a moment that it might just be the years I had been away, but something still made me hold back from approaching. I stood in the road and did not know what to do. In the years away, I had worn out every dream of homecoming, exhausted every fantasy of return. It was my *home*. Until now, it had not occurred to me that they might be gone. But I saw the house and knew at once that it was true.

I retreated a little way down the road. I found a place in the shade to sit. I cannot squat any more, my knee no longer bends as required. I waited, my head dipping towards my chest, my attention given over for a while to the rise and fall of nausea.

I waited a long time, more patient than I had imagined I would be. I sipped slowly from the water bottle Abbas had given me, until it was down to its last drops. Eventually a young man emerged from the door, a woman appearing behind him briefly. They spoke a short while. I did not know them. And then the man left. He did not go to the orchard, but struck out along the road. He walked quickly, as though he were late for something. He saw me, and stared a moment, but he did not come to greet me or ask me who I was. I stayed sitting, and I waited, I am not sure for what. To be welcomed home, returned from the dead. To be recognised, or to see someone I knew. My sisters, my mother, my father. I waited a long time.

I did not see my family. But some people I recognised. Vaguely, across the years. I stood, at one point, to greet a neighbour, a man my father had known. I had waited beside them once, many years ago, an impatient child while they talked. Yet as I took a step towards him, he changed instantly the angle of his path, turning his head from me, continuing on his way. He did not look back. A little later two women passed by, pulling up their veils as they went to cover their faces. They lowered their gazes to the floor. People kept their distance, and would not meet my eye. Only a group of children appeared, a little later, and watched, but they did not show the curiosity we would once have shown, and they did not approach. I felt terribly despondent after this encounter. It is a terrible thing to return home after so long and to be so unwelcome. I retreated from that place, defeated. I thought I was being shunned. I thought that my crimes had been remembered, that those ancient actions still held enough power to leave me an outcast.

Abbas does not think so. Having nowhere else to go, I retreated to his house. The bed was still made for me, and there was food in the kitchen. He sat with me while I ate. I was exhausted from the day, had overexerted myself. It was just rice with dal, but I could barely keep the food down. It seemed to stick in my throat, and my stomach recoiled from it.

I was very upset as I told him what had happened.

'Are you sure you were recognised?' he asked. 'Perhaps they did not look at you long enough to know you. You have been gone too many years and you must have changed greatly. Look how gaunt you are—like a refugee from the war. Your beard! And your paleness: you could be Tajik, or Uzbek, some wild-eyed young man come stumbling across the border. Things are not how they once were. Sometimes those men come, and it is better not to ask who they are, or where they have come from.'

The more time passes the more I am sure Abbas is

right. I have begun to see the evidence. The war has changed everything. In my parents' time they would not have treated strangers in this way. They would have invited them in to rest, would have offered them chai and food, if they seemed hungry. It is *melmastia*, the hospitality our people are known for, the tradition that lives strongly in men such as Abbas. In the mountain passes, the border is fluid and unmarked, and is crossed at will by traders and smugglers, their goods piled high on trains of mules. There were the soldiers, too, who wandered over from Afghanistan for respite from the war, ageing mujahideen warriors who came and stood together in the marketplace, leaning on their rifles. Sometimes they brought fragments of lapis lazuli to sell, and dealers would come from Peshawar, or even Rawalpindi, to bargain over the stones. I remember they looked ancient, some of those soldiers, as old as my grandparents, as though they should be too old to trek in the mountains and fight.

'People are afraid of strangers now,' Abbas said.

'When you found me, I was a stranger, but you were not afraid.'

'I do not wish to damage your pride,' he said, 'but I must tell you, you were not particularly terrifying. Our only topic of discussion was which of our houses was closer, so that you might not die while we carried you there.'

While we talked, Alifa had lingered at the door, a little resentful, no doubt, that I had returned. She is a sweet child, but quite transparent, and given to moodiness. Even I could see that she was annoyed at ceasing to be the centre of attention again. And to have to give ground to such a broken figure, at that. She is used to having her father to herself. She came closer, and began to tug at her father's elbow, until finally, tiring of her attentions, he gestured her gently away.

'Where is her mother?' I asked.

'She died, two years ago.'

'I am so sorry,' I said.

He sighed. 'We had Alifa very late. We wanted more children, but she was ill for so long. It was not possible.'

He left the room briefly and returned from his study with a small framed photograph of his wife. I held the picture briefly before returning it respectfully to his hand.

'She is at peace,' he said.

We sat in silence a while until I felt I could speak.

'Forgive me, Abbas. I do not even know what you do.'

'I keep my house,' he said. 'I raise my daughter. Sometimes I go to the café to play backgammon with my friends.'

I began to explain that I had meant to ask what his profession was, but he interrupted me with a smile.

'I was a poet,' he said. 'A government poet.'

'But now you are retired?'

'Now I have no more poems to write.'

The Orchard

I still feel uncomfortable when I near my old home, and though I have returned every day, I have stayed as far from the house as possible. I do not relax until I have passed from its sight, entering into the privacy of the orchard, shielded by the ranks of its trees. I do not want to know who those people are, living in my home, and I do not want them to know me. And then I have been coming earlier, of course, because dawn has always been the time to come.

I did not stay long this morning. I arrived too late, the dawn already forming around me. In the valley below, the muezzin had begun his call to prayer, the sound of it faint as it reached me, as though it came from a long time past.

I had been too slow to get out of bed. Every part of my body seemed to ache, and when I rolled over I felt dizzy and sick. A terrible nausea curled me into a ball. But still I did not want to miss a day, so I made the walk despite the cramps in my stomach. Several times I had to stop to allow the sickness to subside. My legs felt weak and my breath was hard to catch.

It will be like this for a while longer, I think. I am better than I was, but today even my bones feel ill, as though they have become soft and leprous. I try not to be disheartened by such days, but it is hard when the nausea comes. I tell myself that at least it does not come so severely every morning, and at least, while it does, I am still able to walk. I have come from worse places than this.

In the orchard the irrigation channel is close to dry. It slopes gently down from the lake, higher up the mountain, and either the lake is lower than it has ever been, or, more likely, the narrow channel is blocked by debris accumulated during the winter. I felt distressed to see the meagre trickle of water. It should have been cleared as soon as spring arrived. This was one of my first jobs here, being dispatched up the channel to clear the way, and only if there had been a large slide, if the mud were too thick or the rocks too heavy for me to move alone, would I have to return, and call for my father.

If I arrive earlier tomorrow, and am not so sick, perhaps I will go along and see if I can clear it, just for the pleasure of seeing the water flow.

Beneath the blossom the crowns of the fruit are forming. I can see the beginnings of their flesh, slim and green. Through the summer their shapes will swell and their insides ripen.

So much of my childhood, when my mother allowed, was spent among these trees. My father worked from prayers until noon, when the heat was too much. He moved from tree to tree with his knife, its blade curled like an eyelid, trimming a shoot or branch with practised ease. He saw shapes in the trees that I could not, and brought them forth, making corrections where I could see none that needed to be made.

He owned a radio, which he was proud of—my uncle had bought it for him from the market. Sometimes he would pause from work to clean it of dust, holding it in one hand while he wiped it with the sleeve of his shirt. He listened to the talk stations, mostly. There were voices in the orchard when I worked there. Though I did not really follow the things they spoke of, they were a comforting presence. But still I loved those rare days when he would tire of the conversations and would call to me to change the station, to search the wide static space for some music. I remember dancing to the music one day among the trees, twirling round and round, thinking myself entirely alone until I saw that my father had been watching me. I thought I would be in trouble for not working, but, without altering the seriousness of his expression, he too began to dance, and wordlessly the two of us spun around. He looked so ridiculous that I was overcome by laughter and dizziness, and I collapsed to the floor. He mimicked my fall, throwing his legs above him as he went, and then played dead beside me, his legs rigid and sticking straight up into the air. And yet he was normally so quiet, so careful. When he turned the radio off he would hold it to his ear, checking that the faint electronic hiss had died, anxious to save the batteries.

Even before I was old enough to help him work in the orchard, he brought me here. I remember him swinging me onto his shoulders to carry me proudly through its reach. Together, we were almost as tall as the trees. Often he would swerve beneath them and then stand up on his toes, tangling me in the branches, and causing me to cry out at his clumsiness. Again and again he would play this trick, and I, on his shoulders, with my ankles gripped tightly, could do nothing to avoid getting caught. I would cry with helpless frustration, but the repetition would eventually wear me down, and we would end up laughing.

He laughed almost silently, my father; his face creased and his shoulders shook. Just a faint, delightful wheeze as the air escaped.

How I miss him. This morning I reached for the leaves again, pulling them down to brush against my face. Beneath the dust they are glossy, smooth as polished leather against my cheek.

The Market

Are you waiting for me to tell you that I have missed you, too? Well, I will withhold the thought for a while, until I find words that are sufficient. Let me tell you another story instead; one you will already know.

Do you remember how I introduced myself to you? I would discover, later, that I knew of your family—your father was an assistant political agent for the region, known well beyond the town. I had seen him and your brothers at Friday prayers. Perhaps I even knew there was a sister, though I did not know it was you. I must have seen you many times, when we were children, but all I remember is that first day in the market.

A neighbour's truck had driven me down the hill into town, and I was making my way through the fringes of the market. I carried two heavy bags of fruit intended for a stallholder, the plastic bags stretching beneath the weight, cutting into my hand. I knew to carry them without jolting them, for if the handles broke the bags became impossible to carry, had to be gathered in your arms without the fruit spilling over. I stopped for a moment on my way, placing the bags by my feet so that I could rest my arms. Around me, stalls swelled with walnuts and apples, with grapes and mulberries.

Across the market, I saw you standing against a wall

with your friends. You held the hand of your youngest brother, who stood a little over half your height beside you. You stood at a fruit stall, beside a tray of apricots—I remember because their colour was reflected onto the white silk of your dupatta, a strange trick of the market light. Your kurta, red as the fruits I carried, was embroidered with flowers around the neck.

I did not have the nerve to tell you then. You would have been embarrassed, in any case, and you would have laughed at me. But I have no such fears now, so let me say it: you were so beautiful that I stopped, entirely dumb, in the middle of the street. Your eyes were alive with some inner illumination, a light I had never seen before. I did not know what it was, but it was so pleasurable to me, so exciting. A woman trying to move through the market complained about the obstruction I was causing, and because I was not able to reply, took me for an idiot. She shook her head and berated me loudly as she went past.

I knew I could not say anything to you.

I bent down to my bags, and took from one of them the finest pomegranate I could find. Then I walked up to you, and waited for you to look at me. Your friends stopped talking, and stared at me curiously. Then I held the fruit out at arm's length. I placed its weight in your hand—which you had put out almost in surprise—and then I walked away. I gave you a pomegranate, then I walked away. Your friends, once they had recovered from their amazement, laughed and jeered after me, but I did not turn round. I am sure, I am sure, that you did not laugh with them. Perhaps only a small laugh to cover your embarrassment. I picked up my plastic bags and went on my way. And that was our first meeting.

*

Two weeks later you found me among the fruit stalls. You were carrying your brother. He looked huge in your arms, almost too big for you to lift.

'What is your name?' you asked, and I told you.

'You own the orchard on the hill,' you said.

'It is my father's orchard,' I said, and you laughed, at either my pedantry or my pride. Then you tilted your head to the side, as though weighing something up.

'I am Saba,' you said, and the name seemed like a wonderful gift to me.

It seems so, still. I have carried it for a long time, the most precious thing I owned. I spoke it rarely, so that it would not become tainted by my surroundings. I kept it buried deep inside, and when I had nothing else to cling to, with a single whisper in the dark I would name you, careful not to be heard, and in doing so, something of you would be restored to me, and something of myself would be saved.

The Village

For a long while now I have had no news of my family. You will understand if I say that it was much easier to find news of your father than of my own. His life has been blessed. He is a member of the National Assembly now, a powerful man, more than even he once was. I wonder: do you imagine I am disturbed by this news? It is true, I thought that it would trouble me more. There were times when I wished him to suffer greatly. But they are long gone, and his fate is unimportant to me, in the end. All I wonder is how it has affected you, where it has taken you.

Still, I expressed perhaps too much curiosity about him to Abbas, who warned me that I should be cautious about asking. I could see him wondering what my interest was, but he withheld from asking me. I had wondered for a long time what I should tell him about my past. I was afraid, at first, that he would ask me to leave if I told him about the years in prison, but I came to trust that he would not, and found that my trust was rewarded. He has treated me so well. I am utterly unused to it, and am often at a loss to respond.

He warns me, too, about my daily walks to my old home. He knows that there were old troubles, and thinks I should stay as far from there as possible, though of course he sees me leave every morning, and knows that I am not following his advice. I do not think he knows why I still go. This I keep secret, though I am sure in time he will guess. He is far more intelligent than anyone I have known. And though he is also a kind man, I am afraid he will see only the foolishness of it, the vanity of the act, and not its necessity.

He has offered to help find my family, if I will be patient enough to allow him to look. He does not think it will be difficult. There are few secrets, little that remains unknown. But he warns me that it may take a while, that he will need to ask the questions quietly, and in his own time.

'But we have time,' he says. 'Your family will wait until you are well.'

Recovery comes, though tentatively. It is hard to chart. I do not always feel much better, but I acknowledge, certainly, that I am able to do more than I could even a month ago. In the last week I have begun to help around the house. I am pleased to be well enough, though I am embarrassed to say that I was rather shamed into it. I had been selfish, gathering my energy and hoarding it, expending it only on my morning walks. But now, among other chores, I go every evening to the village well, to fetch water for the house. Formerly, this was Alifa's role, much as it had been my sister's, when I was young. She performed the task uncomplainingly until she realised that I was no longer quite so sick as I had been. I think it came as a surprise to her—as it did, in part, to myself. I am sure she had thought that I was simply a sick person, and not particularly someone who was ever going to get better. But once Abbas had drawn her attention to my improvement, she latched quickly onto it.

'Alifa,' he called, one day, 'isn't our guest looking much better?'

And then that surprise on her face, her mind ticking over. She did not need to think for very long.

'If he is so much better, then what is he going to do? Can he cook? I already do most of the cooking.' This was not entirely true, though she helped her father a great deal.

I shook my head. 'I can learn . . .' I began to say, but realised that neither of them regarded me as a part of the conversation.

'Alifa, my heart, this is no way to treat guests.'

'Then the water!' she said. 'Isn't that a good idea?' she added, pleased with herself.

'Alifa.'

'What? He's bigger than me, he can carry more.' It was her final argument. At which point I stepped in to offer my services—it is embarrassing to be rebuked for laziness by a child—and she folded her arms triumphantly, and her father, annoyed, relented.

I am fortunate it is not far. Two walks each day would be beyond me. I go through the small village, then along the road beside the terraced fields. There are goats and cows, sometimes singly, sometimes in a herd. The people here are mostly farmers. There is however a potter along the street. His workshop is a small open room of the building, with a tarpaulin drawn across the front. By the time I return from my morning walk, the tarpaulin is pulled back, and I can see him at work in the shadows, the steady beat of his foot against the pedal that turns the wheel. Outside the door are lined bowls and tiles, drying in the sun, the clays orange and pink, their grooves perfect, as though the surfaces had been combed.

Only the women of the village collect the water, and if there is anyone there before me, I keep my distance until they are finished. Sometimes I think I see them laughing at me, perhaps making jokes about my presence there. Once, I was greeted by my host's name, and I was puzzled until Abbas admitted that he has told people I am a distant relative of his, come to the mountains to convalesce after a long illness. So at least here, because of this lie, I do not feel unwelcome. The village becomes familiar to me, begins to feel as though it is some kind of home.

How much I have missed village life. I have missed the countryside, the freedom of these surroundings. I have missed the people, and I have missed their goodness; indeed, I had almost ceased to believe in it. And though I had no privacy in the years away, not a moment of solitude, it has only occurred to me lately how lonely I have been.

THE MARKET

How many times did I come to the market to look for you? I took every chance I had to visit the town. After bringing deliveries of fruit I would linger in the places where I had seen you and your friends, would haunt the alleys between your neighbourhood and the market, hoping to intercept you on the way. Once, taking the opportunity to ride on the footplate of a neighbour's truck, I left the orchard without my father's permission. It was a wasted journey—I did not find you that day—and I was beaten when I returned home, but it was not enough to stop me making the trip.

And yet how many times did we meet? Beloved—it cannot have been many. There were days when I found you, and my excitement rose, but the worried look on your face told me that an older brother of yours was nearby, and I should not come to talk to you.

Perhaps our time together amounted to only a few minutes of my life. But they were the most important events I had known, and they expand in my memory to fill the days. Everything was richer for you; the air around us seemed to have some extra colour or intensity to it.

I felt frustrated that we could not be alone. Always, there was your baby brother and your friends. They made jokes about your new peasant friend, said that I came to the market and gave a pomegranate to every girl I liked. It was clear they looked to you for their lead, accepted me only because you did. But they were not unkind.

I felt light in your company. It brought from me a character I was not familiar with. I worked hard to entertain you, to make you laugh. Anything that would cause you to desire even a minute more of my company.

I told you about the orchard. I boasted about it, if I am honest. I told you that it was the most beautiful place on earth.

'Have you been everywhere, then?' you asked.

And of course I had been nowhere.

'No, not everywhere,' I said, attempting to imply that I had seen my share of the world.

'Then where have you been?'

How easily you teased me! So early was it established which of us was the smarter. But I was beginning to learn, and would not be drawn.

'Until you have seen it,' I said, 'you cannot say I am wrong.'

You paused at this. I thought that you were a little impressed by my insistence, though you may simply have been amused.

'Then I suppose I will have to see it,' you said.

The idea seized me.

'Why don't you come now?' I asked.

One of your friends, listening in, gave a sudden, mocking laugh. You looked at me pityingly. I must tell you: before meeting you I had never worried that I was not intelligent. Yet around you, when I most needed it, my mind would not work, and I became quite stupid.

'I am sorry,' I said. 'Forgive me. I did not mean . . .'

But, kindly, you had already changed the subject.

Was this how we came to talk about the wedding? Perhaps I had regained my confidence and was boasting, once again, about the richness of life in our small hamlet. Our neighbour's eldest son was getting married, and they were having a great party at the house. They were the wealthiest of our neighbours, owning the best of the farm-land.

'It is such a shame you will not be there. Everyone from the village is invited. There will be musicians.'

'Who says I will not be there?'

'You don't even know them! How could you be invited?'

'I am coming, with my mother,' you said.

I scoffed, sure that you were teasing me.

'My father is the guest of honour.'

'Your father? Who is your father?'

You watched me carefully as you told me, as though it were a test. But my surprise was not faked, and you shook your head at me, bewildered by my ignorance, and per-haps too, in this one instance only, a little pleased by it. And it was in this way that I came to know who you were.

THE WEDDING

I walked to the wedding party with my father. From the town, guests came up the stream, its bed rocky and dry in the summer, making it a shorter route than the road. We needed only to walk through the trees, and then cut across the field. The corn at head height. I lifted my arms and ran my hands through the ears. As night fell, we went towards the tall mud wall surrounding the house, its gate open. The sky was darkening behind it, a rich blue glow at its heart turning to black. We entered the walled courtyard, and greeted the man of the house. My father was serious in his bearing, earnest and heartfelt in his congratulations.

There were so many people inside. Lit by small fires, the courtyard had corners of dark, patches of brightness. At the front, a group of musicians played, the drums pattering like rain, the strings and pipes weaving among the beat like birds.

I sat on the floor with my father. I do not think he enjoyed these events. He smiled warmly to everyone, but I recognised how uncomfortable he was beneath it, as though he did not feel entitled to be there. He seemed to feel the weight of an obligation to his hosts. I had no such reservations. I was excited, intoxicated by the atmosphere. I saw a group of my friends from the mosque, and went to sit with them and watch the celebrations. When my eyes had accustomed themselves to the lit darkness, I looked for you on the roof that ran around the border of the courtyard, where the women were sitting, gathered around the bride. After a while I saw you, dressed in green and gold.

I looked up at you often, but you were careful not to look at me. Still, I had the sense that each time I turned to you, you had only just looked away. Despite the crowd, I was aware of no one else. It seemed to me that we were the only two people at the gathering, and the party—the noise of laughter and talking, even the music—faded away. An emotion pressing on my whole body. I could hardly breathe.

In the courtyard, the men were taking turns to dance in a space at the front, spinning and leaping as the musicians played, twirling and stomping to the rhythms. The crowd gave money to the best dancers—a show of both wealth and generosity—and the dancers, when they were finished, presented the money in turn to the musicians.

As I sat with my friends and watched, my father leaned forwards and tapped me on my shoulder.

'It is time for you to go to bed,' he said.

It felt as though we had barely arrived. I looked around, and saw no one else leaving.

'Please,' I said. 'A little longer. It is too early. My friends are still here, and they have much further to go than us.'

He relented. 'A little longer,' he said. 'But be ready to leave when I ask you.'

Disappointed, I looked for you, but I had lost sight of you. There was another woman in the place where you had been sitting. I stood up to look around, to see if I could see your mother or your father, but I had begun to feel a sense of panic in my chest, and I saw only a blur of people in the shadows.

I got up from my friends, and went to find my father.

'I am going home,' I said, and he nodded at me. How painful it is to remember. It was the first lie I ever told him, and they were the last words I spoke to him.

I slipped easily through the crowd to the edge of the courtyard. Away from the fires and the press of people the night was cool.

I went as slowly as I could, to increase my chances of finding you. I followed the wall of the courtyard until I came to the foot of a staircase to the roof. I knew I could not go up, and should not be seen lingering there, and when I heard footsteps on the stairs I began to turn away. But I stole a glance as I did so and saw—it felt like a miracle—that it was you, stepping calmly down the steps, your scarf across your face, but dipping low, so that I could see the outlines of your nose and cheeks. I have wanted to ask—was it fate, that you were there? Or had you seen me leave, and come to look for me? I do not think that either answer could be a disappointment. It was so wonderful to see you. All that I had hoped for from the night.

I must have grinned like a fool, but I was not ashamed. Already I knew that love makes fools of us all, and I was satisfied to be as much of a fool as was required.

'As-salaam alaykum.'

'Wa-alaykum asalaam.'

I knew we should not be seen together, that we did not have much time.

'Will you come with me?' I asked.

'Why?' you said.

I thought my heart would break. If you needed to ask why I wanted you to come, then you could not possibly feel as I did. There were no longer any reasons, merely an emotion like an imperative in my chest. Could you not feel it too?

'I must speak with you urgently,' I said.

'Oh, is it urgent?' you said.

By now I was quite frantic, and did not know what to say, but you could not keep your face straight, and a smile broke across it, your eyes flashed, and I felt a burst of joy and triumph. I thought, even then, that I would have to work hard to be worthy of you.

But you looked over your shoulder into the darkness, your expression suddenly worried, and then I too heard someone coming through the dark towards us, and I saw you begin to move away.

'Meet me,' I said, pointing the way across the field. 'Meet me in the orchard.'

THE ORCHARD

I was certain that you would come, and yet fearful that you would not. I remember the fidgeting of my heart. I could not sit still. I leaned for a few moments against a tree, only to jump up as though it were too hot to lean against and had burned me. I walked backwards and forwards along the low wall, balancing on the stones, but then considered that you should not catch me playing a childhood game, and so I skipped down, peering each way into the pre-dawn gloom, my ears pricking at the slightest sound.

It was a child's excitement. My heart is slower now, and waits more patiently.

And then I saw you, approaching tentatively. The night was past its darkest point, but you did not know the path as well as I.

'Saba,' I called, quietly, and you paused a moment. I saw you tilt your head to one side. 'This way,' I said, and you stepped forwards with renewed confidence.

I thought for a moment that you looked uncertain, even embarrassed to be there, but it was quickly covered.

'So this is your famous orchard,' you said. You gestured into the darkness. 'It is everything you promised.'

'You cannot see it now, but it is beautiful in the day.'

'And you expect me to wait?'

'It will not be long. Here, I have brought something to sit on.'

We sat together and talked, shyer than we had been. We talked about things we had not been able to, in moments stolen in the market. You talked about your family and your friends. You told me your favourite colours, your favourite smells.

I felt tired, after the long night, and began to think we could not, after all, wait until dawn. I should not keep you there until then. We would both be in trouble for staying. But I could not bring myself to leave, and you did not ask.

Between the cold of the night and our drowsiness, we drew closer together. And in one moment, which lasted for just a second or two in time, but will live for a lifetime in my memory, you leaned forwards. You pressed your forehead against mine. You rested your cheek by my cheek. And just as you withdrew it, you moved back towards me and kissed me there, your lips pausing a moment, then kissing me again on my jawbone. Truly, I could not imagine that there was a sensation any more wonderful in all of creation.

I kissed your hand, your cheek, and I told you how beautiful you were. It was just for a moment, before you turned your head away. Your hand still tight in mine. I thought my tiredness was gone from me. But when you rested your head on my shoulder, I closed my eyes for a moment, and was somehow asleep.

We woke, later, and watched the dawn arrive. The smudges of grey polished into colour. The sandy path to the village yellowing, and houses emerging from the gloom, their dull mud bricks beginning to warm. The mountains materialising, immense against the skyline, clean-capped with ice, then furrowed and brown beneath the snowline. The cold air somehow lifting, as though the whole valley took in a breath and held it, silent for a moment. It might as well have all been ours to own.

And then the swallows were awake, hunting insects among the trees. They arrowed past in a glide, and then turned with a neat flutter. They dipped overhead, bestowing with their wings a blessing on us.

At my side you were a perfect warmth, a perfect fit.

'There,' I said. 'Is it not as beautiful as I promised?'

And for once, you did not tease me, did not protest, and for a while we watched the dawn together.

Your Father

Saba—we were just children then, and knew nothing of the boundaries that contour the world of adults. We did not know that the world is formed by walls and bars, that peoples are divided from one another. The mountains were porous. How could anyone draw a border there? And if even nations could not be divided, then why should any two people? No, we were children, and knew nothing of this; perhaps we will never be so wise again.

Your father knew those borders. He was a politician, he understood their power. He knew that they could not be crossed without putting the order of the world at risk.

He knew nothing of love, which holds no regard for that order.

When your mother, ready to leave, could not find you at the wedding, he sent one of his servants to fetch you. The man looked for you at the party, but was told you had gone. Someone, certainly, had seen the direction you had left in, and the servant came through the fields and into the orchard to search for you.

Ignorant of this, we slept. The first I knew of it was your cry as you were hauled upwards by one arm. The warmth of you gone from my side in an instant. I stood up to protest, but the man pushed me back down and cursed at me, and dragged you away. A stream of words flowed from his mouth, castigating you for your indecency. He hurried you along, and I began to follow behind, but he turned to shout at me again and I stopped.

Your father would say that we had no business being together, that we belonged to different worlds. But we come from the same earth, you and I, the same people. We speak the same language, drink from the same water tap. We know the same sun, the same sky. So if even we must be divided from one another, what hope is there for the rest of the world?

I Am a Fool

I walked among the trees in a daze. I stopped outside my house, but could not enter. From across the orchard I could still hear the musicians playing, the last of the wedding party determined to see their way through to the next day. My father would have gone home long ago, and have seen that I was not there before him. I would be in trouble for staying out alone, yet I barely thought of it. I turned away and began to walk into town. It was a long way for me then—much longer than my morning walk here—and I had never done it alone.

What was my plan? Did I imagine I would ask you to marry me? I think perhaps I did. Or at least that I would tell your father I loved you, as though the explanation would make everything well.

I know, of course, how foolish I was. I would like to pretend that I was also being brave, but it would be a lie. Let me explain it this way: I felt, simply, as though I had no choice. That life had spoken and I had but one response to it. I smile, though it is bitter, remembering the certainty of youth.

The gate of your garden was open, as though someone had just entered, leaving it ajar behind them. The door, too, was open, and a young woman was sweeping the steps. She looked up from her work, startled, when I greeted her. I spoke your name, asking for you.

She looked at me suspiciously, and I stood tall, pushing out my chest, even though my face burned. Without acknowledging me, she put her broom aside, and went into the house, closing the door so that I would not follow.

My certainty faltered a little, as I stood there. I felt uncomfortably warm, as though my body knew, long before I did, that I should not be there. I tried to plan what I would say, but my mind whirled and would not settle.

From the house I heard the vibrations of speech, deep and quick, and then he appeared suddenly, your father, with a speed that frightened me, causing me to step backwards. He had been woken from sleep—his hair was oily and flattened and his eyes were wide. I opened my mouth to speak, but only a stutter came out. He raised his hand and I felt a bright, sharp pain on my shoulder. It was only then I saw the switch in his hands. A thin cane, the wood pale and slender. I had not seen him holding it. The sting shocked me, and brought tears to my eyes. I was struck dumb by the violence, and could not even protest. Then, when a blow cut a line of blood in my cheek, I screamed. He hit me again and I fell to the floor, and though I curled up the blows continued to fall on my legs, my hip, my back.

I made one last effort to get to my feet and escape, scrambling a short way on all fours, looking behind me to see my pursuer.

But I stopped dead. I saw you standing, open-mouthed, in the doorway.

Your father saw you too. He turned from me and grabbed you by one arm, lifting you nearly from the ground, and then began to beat you, there in front of me.

A sudden fury made me strong. The pain of my wounds

left me. I leapt up and I grabbed your father's hand and tore the switch from it. I could not have been stronger than him, but he seemed so surprised that he did not resist, and stood for a moment in disbelief while with all my strength I struck him on the leg. He flinched and cursed me and tried to seize the weapon back from me, but I struck him hard on his wrist and he howled in pain, cringing away from me, collapsing on the floor as I attacked him again, folding his arms around his head to protect himself. I cut lines of blood into his arms.

I would have ceased, I am sure, or else your father's rage would have overcome his fear and pain and he would have remembered his strength and turned on me. Either way, I would not have killed him, even if you had not stopped me.

You put your hand on my arm. Lightly, but it was enough to restrain me. There was a terror in your voice when you spoke my name.

'Stop,' you said. 'What are you doing?'

You stepped between me and your father. You looked terribly afraid, and I thought you were afraid for your father, worried that I had hurt him, when my own welts still stung.

I became aware of others gathering round us. Our screams had woken the household. Your brothers, bewildered by what was happening, the eldest helping his father from the floor, looking at me in astonishment.

And I was furious at you, that you would choose to protect him, instead of me! I could not contain my anger. I shouted at you. I threw down the cane, and stormed from the house. I walked along the road crying, and the world was blurred by fury and by tears.

I was so young, and so foolish. I am ashamed of my stupidity, and I hope you have forgiven me for it. It did not occur to me that in putting yourself between me and your father, it was me, after all, whom you sought to protect.

The Orchard

As I pick my way uphill my eyes are bent onto the path, and I raise them only occasionally towards my goal. But as I walk home, they are able to roam a little more, and to follow the line of tamarisk bushes along the river far below, a belt of green that leads to where the reed beds open out, their colours brushed alternately with green and yellow as a breeze moves through them. In a distant field a farmer is at work, earlier than usual, walking alongside two oxen, a slow trek back and forth.

Summer is nearly here, and the heat in the middle of the day is brutal. I am cold as I walk in the dawn, but I return in the sun and am vulnerable to it still. I am fortunate the route is all downhill. Yesterday I lay all afternoon in the shade to recover from the exertion.

A few days ago I saw a policeman as I came down from the orchard. He was sitting behind the wheel of a car, parked on the opposite side of the road from me, in the shade at the edge of the village. The car was covered with dust from the roads. It was not a police car, but the man wore his uniform. His sunglasses were mirrors.

I began to shake. My shoulders and arms shook and would not stop. *He is waiting for me*, I thought. It was so early—what other reason could he have to be there? My legs were weak beneath me, and I thought for a moment I would have to stop. It was like a bad dream in which the body refuses to move. My feet dragged when I tried to lift them.

As I drew closer I almost crossed the street to approach him, drawn by some terrible impulse, but some part of my mind was still clear, and I kept to my path. He paid me not the least bit of attention, but I still looked back several times to see if he was following me through the village, if he was watching which way I went. My breath was short, and my heart beat rapidly in my chest for a long time afterwards and would not calm. I felt like a child again.

And yet, all those years ago, when the police first took me, I was not afraid. They came for me as I walked home. I was stumbling slowly, still crying. The pain of your father's blows still burned. I did not understand why you had acted the way you had. I was burning with righteous anger. Had I not tried to protect you?

I was lost in these thoughts, and did not notice the jeep pulling alongside me, or the policemen stepping from it, until one of the men put his hand on my shoulder to stop me. They asked me my name and I told them, and they put me in the vehicle, and we drove to the police station in the town.

At the station they put me in a lock-up, where the warmth of my righteousness was left to cool.

I waited for hours in the cell. It was night before they came. I was taken into a room, bare except for a table and chair. Two policemen were there. I was made to lie on a table, one of the men holding my ankles so that I could not move. The other pulled off my shoes and threw them in a corner. I remember the beginning of my fear. Even after all these years, I remember that this was the moment the fear began. It has not left me since, not entirely. For the first time I thought that the reason my father did not come was that he did not know where I was. Or perhaps he had come there and been turned away, told that he could not see me, or that they knew nothing of me.

They held me down and beat my feet. I had never known such agony—each strike travelling instantly through the entire body, my nerves lit with awful pain. It caused my stomach to seize, and I vomited, almost choking on it before I could turn my head and spit it from my mouth. The policeman swore, and beat me harder. I screamed and screamed. I struggled, but could not move.

They accused me of many things. Of trying to kill your father, trying to steal from him. I told them these were lies but they did not listen to me. They asked me if I had raped you. I did not know what it meant. I grew afraid that I had done something to hurt you, and not known it. That it would explain your anger.

They beat me until I answered yes to all their questions, to the ones I understood and the ones that I did not. I believed I was as guilty as I was made to feel. I wrote my name on blank pieces of paper, without understanding what I was doing.

And then they returned me to the cell. The soles of my feet burned as the blood beat there, bringing crippling waves of pain. I could not stand on them. I lay on my side and curled tightly around myself, and I waited for my father to come and fetch me.

A second night arrived and passed and he did not come. I thought he must be too ashamed to see me, that I had done something terrible. I imagined him angry and disappointed. I felt very foolish. I sat in the cold cell and cried.

By the next morning I was cold. I had not eaten for two days, but the pain made me sick to my stomach and I felt no hunger. No one had come during the night, and I looked up in hope when the door screeched open. One of the policemen came in and I craned my neck to look for my father behind him, waiting outside. I did not see him; he was not there. Without warning, the policeman hit me hard over my head with his baton. I was unprepared, and fell to the ground, shocked. Blood dripped from my eyebrows, and I raised my hand to my forehead. My arm felt light; the world seemed to vibrate.

He pulled me from the lock-up. My legs would not hold beneath me, and so I was dragged along the corridor and into the sun. My face was wet, and through the blood and bright light I looked around stupidly for my family.

I was lifted from the ground and thrown into the police jeep. The door slammed behind me. Even then I thought I would be taken home, the violence I had inflicted on your father already repaid tenfold. But the engine started and the vehicle rolled forwards, out of the yard and turning right, heading further down the valley, away from my village, away from home, and everything that was left in my heart descending with us.

*

'Where are we going?' I asked the driver.

The policeman sitting beside him laughed.

'Did you hear that?' he asked. 'He wonders where we are going.'

He leaned back over the seat. 'Where do you think we are going? We are going for a nice day out! We are going to have a picnic.' He laughed at his joke.

I put my hand to my forehead. The cut no longer ran and the blood was clotting, but I felt nauseous, and the wound was a vicious, persistent throb. I could feel the thin split flesh, the open bone.

A few minutes later the man turned back to me, his voice calm and serious. 'You assault a girl, and then attack her father. Don't you know he is a very important man? So we are taking you into the desert to shoot you.' He leaned sideways to show me the gun in his holster, the metal and leather smart and black, snug against his belt. 'Bam! Like this. It will be over quickly.'

They did stop, on the way, at a deserted roadside, and I was terrified. I huddled against the seat, expecting the door to be thrown open. I began to panic. My hands searched for something to hold on to, and my fingers tightened on the seat belt, prepared to hold on with every bit of my strength. But they did not come for me—the driver stood with his back to the car, relieving his bladder, and when he was done he got back in the car without looking at me. In a minute we were travelling again.

The car threw up dust from the road, which swirled in through the windows. It filled my mouth and my thirst was tremendous.

'Please,' I said, 'may I have some water?'

I was ignored. We drove further and panic began to set in. I did not know where we were, had never travelled so far. I craned my neck to look back the way we had come, trying to remember the turns we had made, but I had not been paying attention, and I was lost.

'I am thirsty,' I said. 'You must give me water!'

Again I was ignored, and so I shouted louder. I demanded to know where they were taking me. 'Where is my father?' I shouted. My fear left me, and I became reckless. What did it matter, if they were going to kill me? I screamed at them until the jeep stopped again, and the door gaped open and hands reached for me. I felt the sharp roadside stones on my palms and knees, and then a baton hard and crippling on my thigh, a heavy boot in my ribs.

I curled into a ball for the remainder of the journey. I remember the sickness more than the pain. It caused deep groans to well up from my stomach, but I quieted them, moaning to myself beneath the engine noise.

THE GARDEN

It is the afternoon, and I am resting in the garden, recovering from my walk this morning. It is so pleasing to be able to rest here. When I first rose from my bed and went to sit outside, I needed Abbas's help to move. He placed my arm around his shoulder and almost carried me at his side. I was so light I think he could have lifted me with a single arm. Alifa skipped ahead of us, impatient to show me her corner of their garden. After so many days in that bed, after so many years of longing for light and space, I could not have been more disenchanted. I thought I had replaced one cell for another. The walls of the garden hemmed me in. It seemed a small place, and only the blue roof of it, impossibly high above, reminded me that I was no longer imprisoned.

I sat on a step in the shade, and it was a long time before the beauty of the place came to me. I do not think I saw it at all at first. My eyes could not focus on the gentle order Abbas had created, or on the flowers Alifa was naming. The vision was overwhelming. I saw nothing but a jumble of colour. I saw nothing but the walls. I felt dizzy, and I bent forwards over my legs, my head down, waiting for my trembling fit to stop. I breathed deeply. I wanted only to return to the bed I had been so glad to get out of. I bent over, burrowing back inside myself.

And yet as I breathed, I became aware of a strange sensation growing inside me, some force that seemed to swell
from my chest and then spread through my body like an
energy. I felt almost faint. I was stunned by it. I did not
know what was happening.

'What is that?' I said, reeling.

'What's wrong?' asked Abbas. His concern was quiet,
but urgent. He put a hand on my shoulder to steady me.

I could not explain it. I waved my hands around in the
air to try to communicate. And suddenly he seemed to
understand. His face seemed sad and pained. When he
spoke, his voice was low.

'It is the roses,' he said.

'No, no . . .' I began. I thought I had not explained
myself.

But to my amazement, I realised that he was right. It
was the scent of roses, the smell faint but so sweet, and it
came to my dulled senses as powerfully as any narcotic.

I sat there for a long time until the shade had moved
from me and I felt the warmth of the sunlight on my skin.
My sensitivity was such that it prickled and brought a rash
which lasted for days, but I would not move when Abbas
tried to bring me in.

'You should take care,' he said. 'The sun will still be
here tomorrow.'

'A little longer,' I said. 'Please. I want to feel it now.'

I have come to love the garden since then, and I think
that my time resting outside, shaded from the sun but
enjoying the warmth, my skin alert and alive to the slightest breeze of air, has been the equal of any of the medicines
I was given. Alifa tells me about the roses and I allow my
eyes to linger on their colour. Abbas explains to me a little

of the different plants he grows there, the flowers and herbs, and I begin to appreciate the carefulness of his arrangement, and how the stone wall shelters them, allows them life.

On the left-hand side, in one of the thick streams of mortar that affixes the stones of the wall, a script flows, carved in beautiful handwriting. The alphabet is familiar to me, but the words are foreign. It is Persian, Abbas has told me, a line of poetry that reads: '*If there is a paradise on earth, it is this, it is this, it is this.*' He told me that this word, *pairidaeza*, is from the old Persian, and originally referred to a walled area, a garden. So in my first weeks in this place I have come to understand that not all enclosed spaces are prisons, and that some are for safety: some are sanctuaries.

*

I am sitting there now, as I write, sheltering from the afternoon sun. Alifa is playing a game in the doorway, which seems to require her jumping with both feet across the entrance, first this way, and then that. She had been playing indoors until her father berated her for making too much noise, and sent her outside. I think she has become accustomed to my presence in her home now, and rather than seeing me as competition for attention, slowly begins to regard me instead as another source of it.

'What are you playing?' I ask.

'I have to cross the river without getting wet.'

'But why don't you swim?'

'I don't know how to swim.'

'Neither do I,' I confess.

Her jumping continues for a while, and I write to the sound of bare feet slapping lightly against the ground. She counts under her breath as she leaps. When I become aware that she has grown quiet again, I look up, and see her standing there, watching me.

'What are you writing?' she asks.

'I am writing stories,' I say.

'Will you tell me one?'

I look down at my notebook.

'Not one of these. Perhaps I will write something else for you, later.'

The answer seems to satisfy her and she returns to her game.

How strange it is to be resting here, acutely aware of the fragrance of the flowers in my nostrils and watching a child play in the doorway of her home, yet turning my mind to such dark places. There are things about which it is hard for me to write. I own impulses that are difficult to reconcile. I want to tell you what has happened to me, but there is a stronger force, something akin to shame, that seeks to compel me to keep quiet, to push the story deep within and bury it in the darkness. This, my body tells me, is the easier course. But I do not trust this urge, and so although it is hard, I will tell you the story, as best as I am able, and I will tell you about:

The Prison

I will tell you about it because I want you to know the places I have been. It causes me pain to think that you know nothing of my life. It is a selfish desire, I know, one I trust you will forgive me for. Above all, you must understand that I do not want you to think that I suffered because of you; I did not. You could never cause me to suffer. There is evil in the world, which finds us all, and which did not arise from you and me.

The prison they took me to is many miles from here. A long way south, in the plains. The earth has a different colour there; the sand is paler. But I saw little of it. Our cell was a concrete room with a low ceiling. There were raised concrete slabs with holes drilled into their sides so that we might be chained to them. I was not able to stand up in that room for a long time. The chains were heavy, and dug deeply into my skin where I had to lie on them. There were ten such slabs, in two close rows, but sometimes the men in the room numbered eleven, or fourteen, or seventeen, and those who had no slab were squeezed onto the floor between them, and chained there.

My first memory is of the smell. I was confused when I arrived, and in great pain from the beatings, but as they carried me into the room the stench of it woke me, and I tried to push back against the men who carried me. The air was thick with sickness and feces and sweat and I could not stomach it. On the first day I retched constantly, my stomach heaving dry until I was vomiting only air and saliva. I sought to expel the taste from my mouth, but eventually I had no spit to summon. The smell clung to my dry throat, and seemed to penetrate every part of me. It saturated everything. It is true that, in time, one grows used to such things, but even as the body becomes accustomed to it, it learns the smell so completely that it becomes impossible to forget. The sensation is overwhelming, and allows nothing else to stand. Until that day in Abbas's garden, when I first became aware of the roses, I had forgotten what it was to have a sense of smell. Even now, despite the slow healing of my senses, some mornings I awake to find it thick in my nostrils and full in my mouth, and I am filled with horror until I realise where I am, and the reek, which was merely a phantom of my mind, evaporates.

It was worst in the heat of summer, and if there were many of us chained against the rough floors it became hard to breathe the stifling air. Only rarely were we taken out into the yard. Inside, we lay still, and tried to breathe slowly, deeply. It was a relentless suffocation. A single small window, barred over and set high in one wall, was the only ventilation. But in the winter nights, unprotected by blankets and with only thin prison shirts to cover us, we would shiver and freeze.

The place was a nursery for sickness. The water we were given was meagre and filthy, and the toilet was an uncovered hole in one corner, layered around in feces. We lived with rats and flies. Over the years I was ill constantly, and there was no medicine for us. Within days my body was covered in a rash and at night the itching was unbearable, particularly on the soles of my feet where I could not reach it. I rubbed them against the floor to ease the awfulness, though it sometimes made it worse. I pulled against the chains, so that the pain of it would distract me from the itching. In the places I scratched it, my skin thickened into crusts, until my face carried the same scarring I saw on the other prisoners, scabs the colour of honey collecting over our chins and around our noses.

My family did not come. The hope that they might lived for a long time in my heart, until I knew at last that it deceived me. A hard truth, in the end, is not so cruel as false hope. And though I blamed myself for my foolishness, I came to understand that they did not come because they were prevented from doing so, or because they did not know where I was. I knew my father. However much I had displeased him, he would not have abandoned me. But it is easy for powerful men to do these things, to make their enemies disappear, even if their enemies are children. Perhaps they were told the same lie the policeman had told me: that I would be killed. Perhaps they mourned for me, said prayers for me. Perhaps they petitioned for my body to be returned, so that they might bury me.

THE PRISON

Above all else, the prison taught me that there are evil men in the world. It is in all of us, perhaps—I do not think anyone knows what they might do, should they find themselves in extreme circumstances. No one can say that they would not do wrong. There are places that cause wicked thoughts and actions to arise unbidden in everyone who goes there. But this is not all. There are men, too, who seem to have been born without the capacity for remorse, and for whom pleasure exists only in causing suffering to others.

Of the men I knew in prison, some of them, in time, were kind to me. Some even became my friends—but later, much later. I first needed to know that in order to trust, you must learn to distrust. When I arrived I was too young, too soft to be anything other than a victim. What could I have imagined of evil, with the childhood I had known?

My initial lesson came in the form of a man, Saleem Mahmood. He owned factories in Mardan and Peshawar. He had killed a man, one of his own workers, after a disagreement. Had followed him home after an argument, the story went, and killed him at his own door. He was in the cell when I arrived, and it was soon clear that it was his space I had been brought into.

I was a child then. Weak, and ignorant of the things men could do to one another. I am sure he saw my weakness clearly. He befriended me and told me that he would protect me, that I would need a friend if I were going to survive. He took pleasure in control. Took pleasure in playing games in this way, in building up my trust, and then, through unspeakable acts of violence, destroying it. I will not speak the words. I was at the mercy of that man for too long.

In the end, my only good fortune was that he was not among us for long. He had too much money, friends who would pay for his release as soon as a minimum time had been served. I do not mean to compare him to your father—the two men are not alike—but there was one aspect only that was familiar to me. He had no turn of anger, as your father does—his calmness was terrifying—but even in his chains he had an aura of power to him. A sense that the world would be as he willed it. And he willed the world to be a dark place: he manipulated others into suffering so that something in him might be satisfied.

*

It was not only the other prisoners. The guards, too, beat us, and because of the chains we could not defend ourselves.

Sometimes they would unchain us and take us to another room, where we would be tortured. They held our arms behind our backs, pulling them into positions which were unbearable to hold and tying them tightly. My arms and back still ache, the muscles and tendons forced into forms they were not meant to take. For the remainder of

my life there will be something about me that is mis-
shapen. Sometimes they would hang us from our ankles
and use a reed to cut into the soles of our feet. Or while we
hung, they would take wires from a battery and apply
them to our chests or our bellies, or our genitals, to see
how we spasmed, to see how we twisted. To hear our
groans, sounds wrung up from the deepest pits of our
insides. I remember biting my tongue once, and the blood
filling my mouth, pouring into my throat and nose so that
I could not breathe, but even as I choked, the shocks still
came and my nerves still writhed.

Every instinct of the body is to recoil from pain, but
they allowed us no escape. An awful sense of powerless-
ness grew steadily, as though I were inhaling a great breath
of air and was unable to stop. The horror became overwhelming, and from some hidden place in my mind I felt
a darkness, something huge and unnameable, begin to
form.

Even a few minutes of torture seem to last forever. I
remember strange details. The smell of paan on their
breath. A pair of metal pliers on a table top. I can still picture them, and the thought comes with a shiver: their steel
was blackened and tarnished, rust speckled like a lichen at
the hinge. Willing it all to be over. Thinking that yes, I
could bear this moment, this pain, perhaps the next, if
only they would stop. And then an agony would squirm in
my body again and I would be lost, only slowly returning
to my senses. I would wonder how many days I had been
tormented, only to find, on being returned to the cell, that
I had been gone no more than an hour or two.

At the beginning, I thought that they did this to punish
me for what I had done, and so for a while I accepted the

pain. How unfaithful my heart would be if it failed you now, if it felt that you were not worth the suffering. I asked the men to forgive me.

But the guards did not discriminate between the prisoners. They seemed to choose one or another of us almost on a whim. They did not call us by name, did not rebuke us for our crimes, and I came to understand that they were not punishing us. They did not care who we were, or what we had done. Their actions were guided by neither justice or retribution, nor even by malice, but by something far more banal, far more terrible. Simply, they were bored. They subjected us to appalling tortures, roused terror and agony in our eyes just so that they might be briefly relieved of the boredom of their jobs, and to remind themselves that they were not like us, that the time we spent in the prison was theirs, laid claim to, and could be controlled as they wished.

This knowledge was shattering to me. I had withstood the first weeks because I believed there was an order to things, whether that order was just or unjust. That my suffering continued even after I had understood its senselessness, its absurdity, was a terrible blow. The darkness I had felt forming inside rose up, immense, and engulfed me. I had no defence against it. It was such an unspeakable thing; I feel as though I have known it as intimately as I could, and still I do not have the words to explain its horror. If, at first, I had struggled against my lack of freedom, like a bird beating its wings on its cage, then that struggle lessened and finally ceased, and a stagnant resignation came upon me. I registered very little. My body became filled with disgust for itself.

I thought of you, but my thoughts were damaged. I

conjured you, imagining you stepping among the prisoners, coming to lie beside me, to stroke my wounds and hold my head. You were my only recourse, the only thought that brought relief to my mind, and I thought of you constantly, until I understood that I did not want you in that place, that I should keep you from it, and save you only for the quietest, most desperate moments in the dark of the night, when you could walk through the room unseen and remain uncontaminated by it. You were the only good in my life, and I protected your name as though it were a sacred thing.

Trying now to remember all this is hard. The order of events is confused. I cannot pull the years apart, and arrange them as they fell. I know that there came a time when the memory of you alone was not enough to save me. I thought I would not see you again, and your visits, in my mind, began to bring more pain than they eased. The darkness consumed me. My mind was black. I began not to care if I lived, and then after a while I began to long, more and more forcefully, to die: every part of my body yearning for it, for the relief of death. The need persisted for so long that it wiped almost every other desire from me. I needed to be free from the prison, saved from the punishments, and it seemed the only exit. If there had been an easy way, a sure way, I would have taken it.

*

Even these memories begin to cloud. They are horrific, but they do recede. It is a strange thing, because I thought the intensity of those times would always be with me. I almost feel as though I should hold on to it, to remember what was done to me. But though we are built to heal, or at least to survive, to forget, suffering has inscribed patterns of thought deep into my mind, and I think that some of the damage will not heal, even after the memories are long faded.

THE NOTEBOOK

How I love this paper! Abbas gave me this notebook. He had bought several of them for Alifa to use at school. There was a pile of them at the end of one bookcase. He came in one day to find me holding one of the books, turning it over in my hands, running my fingers, their tips still scarred from burns, over the rough surface.

'Do you read and write?' he asked me.

'A little,' I said. I had not written since I was a child. The only text I had read was the Qur'an.

'Did you go to school?'

'No. I learned at the mosque. We had classes sometimes, after prayers.'

'Show me,' he said. 'Perhaps you can help Alifa with her school work.'

And then later, after I had tried to make my broken hands control the pen, had struggled to form letters that once came easily: 'Or perhaps Alifa can help you.'

I have had to learn again how to write. I had almost forgotten, and it was painful to grip the pen in my hand for any length of time. My thumb tingled with numbness, and my palm would freeze in agonising contortions so that I had to massage my grip free. But my two teachers, one old and one young, have been patient with me, and my long-ago lessons had not left me entirely. I was soon able to sit and write with Alifa. It is true that my hand still aches as I work, that I must pause often and stretch my fingers before I take up the pen again, to allow the cramps to fade, but the process of adding words to the page brings so much pleasure that I do not mind the discomfort that accompanies it. In the cold morning air it takes a minute before the ink in my pen flows, and I write with it against the skin of my arm until it comes, not wishing to deface the pages of the notebook until I can write on them cleanly.

And, yes, the notebook: its covering card is dyed violet, like the sky at dusk, at the last moment before darkness. Its paper is handmade, mulched together and pressed down then dried in the sun, before it was cut into sheets and folded into books. The pages bear the marks of their construction, and recorded in the texture of each page must be some evidence of the individual who made them. Within the paper are fine flecks of chipped wood, and threads run beneath the surface like the fossilised remains of creatures that we used to find in the rocks, in places along the roadside. The firm tip of my ballpoint pen travels pleasurably over them. Along the spine, three holes have been pierced with an awl, and the loose leaves are tied through them with rough string. The string is long, so that it may be wrapped around the book to bind it; it trails loose now, as I write in the opened leaves.

It is a wonderful luxury to own, and the greatest pleasure of my day is to sit down with it, whether in the orchard or here in the garden, and write a little. Sometimes I stop to smooth my hand across the sheet, over the new thread of ink, and my attention settles for a moment on the physical details of the page, on the paper, its beauty and solidity, and I find I have drifted away into thought, losing myself for a while, and when I wake it takes several moments before I remember where I am, or how I came to be here.

*

How easily these days pass. The months are wearing lightly; I hardly feel them as they go. After the slowness of time in prison, it is a shock. No longer unbearable, time has become a comfort, as soft as a blanket. I could sleep it away and still be satisfied. Abbas has been encouraging me to use my time to read, as well as write—he thinks it will lessen the boredom of recovery—but the truth is that I am not bored. Boredom is something I no longer experience. It is gone from me, lost during those years of enforced stillness. I could watch the sky all day, and breathe the air, and never once grow tired of it. It is enough, more than enough, not to suffer.

In any case, I could not read for long to begin with, but as my stamina has returned, so have the headaches lessened. Reading comes more easily now. Abbas has so many books in his study, more than I have ever seen. Varnished wooden shelves cover two of the walls, from floor to ceiling, and they are full of books written in many languages. I cannot believe he has read them all.

'How is it possible to read so many?' I ask him.

'You begin with one,' he says. 'And then you move on to the next. And *insha'Allah*, your life will be long.'

In his house are works of history and philosophy, and many books of poetry. Some bear his name, though they are too difficult for me to follow. In any case, the books I like best are those on nature. I have read his gardening books, which are filled with beautiful pictures of flowers I do not recognise. He even has a book written in English which tells you about all the birds, and though the alphabet is foreign to me, with the help of the pictures, and with Abbas as translator, I have been learning as much as I can.

Saba, beloved, let me tell you about:

THE SWALLOWS

I would never have believed there were so many different kinds, until I looked in that book. There are pages and pages of them, so many that I was confused, and did not know which of them represented *our* swallows; if they were the ones called *red-rumped*, or perhaps *streak-throated*.

But I persisted, and looked in greater detail, and finally among the pictures I saw one with a blue mask across its eyes and a rusty crown to its head, and I know now that the swallows that arc among the trees in our orchard are known as *wire-tailed*. Their tail feathers are long, you will remember, like fine threads trailing their flight, as though they were at the end of a long kite string, only the furthest filament visible as it glints in the sun.

According to the book they are solitary birds, and so I suppose that it is unusual to see as many as we have here. They nest near water, and must therefore come to the orchard from the lake, perhaps along the irrigation channel, tracing their way along the ribbon of water to feed on the insects that buzz among the trees.

They have become accustomed to my presence here in the morning. They flash white and blue as they swoop and veer ever closer, so that sometimes I hear only the distinct flap of a wing beside my ear as one turns over in mid-flight, changing direction impossibly to swerve around me. They are so quick, so perfect in their lines, like little miracles in the air.

One day, when I lay in the prison cell in a stupor, my eyes unfocused on the ceiling, I saw a flutter of the light at the window. I am not sure how long I had been there. Many months, certainly, though it might as well have been a lifetime. It was in my mind's darkest weeks. But the flutter of light: I have told you that the window was small, and high on the wall, and from where I lay I could not see the sky. Yet there was that flicker there, as though the sun were a bulb losing its electricity, or a candle guttering in the breeze. Too sudden, too complicated, to be a cloud. Perhaps I had seen it many times, without once thinking of its significance. This time, however, something deep inside woke up, the first stirring of an old familiarity. So I kept my eyes on the window, and the slant of light it cast against the wall, waiting for the flicker to repeat. And when it did I saw a shadow pass, too quick to leave a shape.

Alert now, I rose into a sitting position. I knew what it was. I knew, but my mind would not remember. I sat for a long time, my brain reaching for something just beyond it, until the feeling of familiarity grew and became overwhelming, until at last I was able to name what I had seen as a bird, and I was sure, simply sure, that it was the exact flutter the swallows made, as they reached a perch. A dipping and braking, a folding of their wings as they landed.

There were swallows nesting in the eaves of the prison wall. It was frustrating not to be able to see them, but I pictured their nests, neat bowls lined with mud. They were not the same swallows I knew, and I thought for a while that perhaps they were just swifts or martins. But sometimes in the yard I would catch a glimpse of one looping over the top of the wall, and I was able to recognise it.

And on those occasions thereafter, when we were taken from our cells and made to march, chained, around the dusty yard, I would crane my neck upwards, blinking into the light, looking for the swallows. I would trip, often, holding up the march, and be beaten for my trouble, told to watch my step. But I could not watch the ground. My eyes strained upwards, greedy for a sight of the birds, even if they flew high and were only dark specks against the blue. And when I raised my head and saw them flying free there was the feeling in my heart of something I had not known for a long time. It was joy, and it was the most painful thing I have ever felt, because it reminded me of everything we no longer owned. But now I had two visitors to my prison: you, in the secret moments, and the swallows. Two secrets to protect, two poles to hold on to, and so balanced, a hope began to rise that I might survive the days.

The Orchard

The monsoon is here. It does not fully reach us, high in the valley. But the air has become more humid, and from the mountainside I can see the clouds, low and heavy on the distant plains. It is a strange season to be walking, the land so dry one day, and then the next, half the road will have been washed away by a sudden downpour.

I wonder, as you read this, what you think of me. Of my calmness. Do I sound reconciled to everything that happened? Do I sound as though I have no anger?

Listen: I knew a man in prison, Ibraheem Jamal. He was tall, and soft with wealth when he arrived with us, his flesh heavy on his body. He sweated copiously in the heat, his shirt soaked and his forehead bright. He had been convicted of murder, though he was dismissive of the charge. It was a false accusation, he said, brought by a family with a feud against his own. He was made hostage by his imprisonment until a financial disagreement could be settled. Perhaps what he said was true; there were other men in the prison with similar stories. The guards did not treat him unjustly.

From the moment he entered our cell he spoke angrily about his enemies, about those who he believed had plotted to destroy him.

'I have killed no one,' he said. 'But they have turned me into a killer.'

He was consumed by fantasies of revenge. In the night he would mutter to me their crimes and the violence he would do to them in return. He recited the details of imagined punishments with a fervour that disturbed me. It was like a physical thing inside him, and it consumed his mind. Another man told him to trust in Allah, who would repay his enemies for their sins. But Ibraheem Jamal raised his finger, which shook with anger as he held it close to the man's face. '*Every wrong is avenged on earth*,' he said.

So, among the powerless, do dreams of power proliferate. Within two years the prison broke him. He was released, but the man who left was unsound. Physically, he had suffered: his once-full frame was gaunt and the skin of his torso hung wrinkled and loose. But more than this, he had become a darkened shadow of a man, paranoid and distrustful. He believed we conspired against him, that we sought to poison his food. His moods were unpredictable, switching in an instant from friendliness to violence. His obsession had undone him; his dreams had constructed a new world, and he had gone to inhabit it. He saw this world everywhere, and reality escaped him.

It is true that I, too, was angry for a long time, first at those whom I blamed for my imprisonment. My hatred for your father tormented me for years. And in my confusion I was also angry with my family, for not seeking me out, and I was angry with you, too, for not pleading with your father to find out where I was. I could not believe it possible that you knew, and yet could not persuade him to take pity on me. I understand now, of course, that even if you had known, you could have done nothing.

The anger has faded. I have no desire to seek revenge. I do not think it was anything I did. I think, simply, that I was just fortunate that my rage did not overwhelm me. Perhaps I came to understand that it was not real. And as I write to you, the last of my resentment is subdued. I seek only peace. I seek to be better than the person I am.

I do not even regret that I was imprisoned. It would be senseless to do so: our lives are leaves, and the wind takes them where Allah wills. The days fall as he allows, and this I accept. But I do still regret, for one reason only, the years. I regret them because we were apart, because I was not with you, and everything that might have been between us was never allowed to be. I regret, because we cannot have the time back.

Perhaps you will think me foolish. Perhaps you have put the past behind you, and whatever regrets you might have had have been set aside, because you do not see their purpose. Time softens all griefs, they say, and it is useless to dwell on lives that might have been. We are granted only one life, and one life is enough. Whom do such regrets profit? What do they achieve, except to bring us unhappiness?

Listen: I feel regret because love is priceless, and because I do not wish to deny it its value. Because I know what might have been, had you and I been together. How I still long for those years! They were taken from us, and can never be returned. But they are precious beyond measure, and I will be loyal to the love I have felt for you, and will not lay it aside. If I did not feel regret, I would forget its value; I would keep nothing of its worth.

Every day I long for something I will never have, and I am learning to live with that longing. Is this not better than forgetting—to face our regrets for what they are, to know their measure, to know the value of what we have lost?

The Waterfall

Do you remember in the marketplace, at the corner of the square, the area where they sold birds? The narrow walkways formed by cages piled high, each packed with so many birds—twenty or fifty or a hundred. The musty, feathered smell, their deafening song. As a boy, I was thrilled by them, by the noise and scratching life as I swept through there with my friends. We would run our hands along the rough cages, feeling the metal vibrate and the birds react, and then the merchant would shout at us and we would scatter. Or we dared each other to push our fingers into the holes, to be pecked by the birds. Always one of us would be scratched or bitten deeply enough to draw blood, and sometimes tears.

At the edge of this area, at the entrance to the market on that side, where people came past, a fortune-teller had a table. A parrot perched on it, because it was believed that such birds knew the future. For a few rupees, the fortune-teller would lay out his cards and the bird would pick one. I thought nothing of it then, but I remember now how the bird was held to the table by a small plastic tie, fed through the table surface and pulled tight over one of its claws. If it is true they can see the future, then I pity them for their own. No living thing is meant to be caged.

Time slows in such circumstances. The days became

endless, and illness or punishment caused them to be slower still. There were terrible nights that seemed to last forever, nights when I would think I had slept, and then wake, either because of the heat or nausea, to find that only a few moments had passed. I would wake a hundred times in one night, the dawn no nearer. But in compensation for the horror of hours, the body also slows. My heartbeat weakened to a faint pulse. I withdrew into myself and my thoughts widened, expanding into the empty spaces. They came as slowly as the glaciers of the Hindu Kush descend from their heights.

In that first summer I lay on the floor in a torpor, barely breathing and dreaming my dazed thoughts. The air was so thick none of us had enough energy to move even a limb. Our mouths were dry and our heads ached. Memories of my family, and thoughts of you, tumbled together until I drifted, lost in them, without any sense of where I was. I spent hours and then days in that state, my consciousness submerged, not coming up for air. Over the years I would see how some of the prisoners retreated further into those places, leaving a little more of themselves behind each time. They became inhabited by some vacancy, as though some crucial part of them was gone, and I did not want the same to happen to me.

In time I learned to discipline my thoughts, to make my memories precise. I started by remembering the people I knew, calling them to me, imagining them standing above me. To see their clothes and their gestures, to hear their voices speak to me. I heard them say my name. My mother's voice, calling me from the orchard. I thought of my father, his moustache beginning to grey, and the lines on his face creasing as he smiled. I conjured his farmer's hands, grooved from work and dusted with earth, reaching down to lift me up, to pull me free from the chains.

There is a nakedness to imprisonment. No part of yourself can remain hidden. Our lives, our characters, are opened and stripped. But still, in the darkest times I pictured you stepping silently through the door, your feet treading easily among the bodies, too light to wake them. I fought to remember your face, and when it would not come, I remembered the feel of your head on my shoulder, your lips on my cheek. You were my last secret, the first pole of my survival, and I would not give you up.

And then, when the heat became unbearable, I would imagine the waterfall. I would remember how, following our lessons at the mosque, my friends and I would walk up to the road above the village, where a glacial stream ran. When the road was built, the workers cut sharply into the hillside, leaving a tall cliff. The meltwater, coming down the slope, had worn into the rock face, creating a cleft with a pool at its base. On the hottest days the water was still icy, and well worth the long walk uphill.

I made that journey in my mind many times. I remember the bank at the edge of the village, how it took a short run up to reach its top. I felt in my chained legs the extra weight of those four or five steps, the sudden rise as we crested. I remember how the path looked from there, running up the hill, cutting first to the left, and then turning sharply and running to the right all the way up until it joined the road. How the dirt of its surface turned to shale higher up, which slid beneath our feet. I picture the mazri bushes growing on the hillside, spilling from the sandy soil. How as we neared the road our climb became a race, one of us at first walking a little faster to try to gain some ground, and then the rest of us responding, pushing at each other for position, beginning to run, as a group at first, but then the swiftest breaking away from those who were slower or younger, until whoever had most strength in their legs reached the top and stood on the road, looking down triumphantly upon those who had needed to stop to catch their breath. I can hear the quick, excited breaths of my friends around me, their half-shouts and laughter, I can feel their shoulders against mine, and on my hands I can feel the stones when I slipped and pushed against the ground to steady myself.

Having no brothers, I revelled in the company of my friends. I had no fear as a child; I was the bravest of us, the first to clamber onto the rocks, the first beneath the icy water to feel its weight beat on my shoulders. You will think me boastful, but how can you deny it, when I was brave enough to approach you that day in the market?

I could not swim—I do not think that any of us had ever learned—but the pool was not deep, and if the waterfall pushed you beneath it, it was only to hold you for a moment against the smooth rock at the bottom, and then to release you, pushing you quickly into the shallows. Or we would employ the trick I had once seen my uncle perform, which was to tie his shalwar kameez tightly at the wrists, ankles and waist, and wade into the water. When wet, the baggy fabric kept air inside, and he could lie back and float easily, bobbing high in the water.

I do not feel brave any longer. That overconfident, sociable child has grown to be a guarded, solitary man. I cling to those memories of playing with friends because they are the last memories I have of childhood. The boy I once was is a stranger to me, and sometimes I wonder if terrible experiences are enough to change a person—I mean fundamentally to change a person's nature—or if they merely subdue it, and it endures there beneath, and will reassert itself in time. I wonder if I will be recognised by my family. If those I love will still know me.

I think of my old friends often. Even in my freedom I have retraced that same journey many times, until the memory has become worn from use, and the features of my friends, like stones beneath a waterfall, have been smoothed into indistinctness. Sometimes in my dreams I see a glimpse of a familiar face, as though it were turning to me, but in a second it is gone and when I wake I cannot bring it to mind, no matter how hard I try.

THE PRISON

I grew accustomed to imprisonment—perhaps too much—to its rules, its systems. It became the only life I knew. Even now, it is hard to shake. The laziness that Alifa sees in me is not only tiredness, but also habit, deeply ingrained. I find it hard to stir myself to action, and I am nervous at the thought of change. I want things to remain as they are, without upheaval. My body shakes and my heart beats when I think of leaving here. There is too much that is unknown, too much that I cannot control.

I think I have told you that I had friends in prison. Men I liked, whom I talked with through the long days. I wonder if I will see them again. Sometimes there were other children, too, and my closest friend in the cell, for the months he was there, was a boy named Karim. He arrived in the night, and I was woken twice, first by the pulling of chains as he was brought in and locked beside me, and then again, a few minutes later, by a poking in the ribs.

'Hey,' he whispered, 'if we're going to spend time all cosy together, then we should get to know each other, no? You've got a lot to catch up on.'

I was years older than him when he was brought into the jail, but he seemed to have lived a hundred lives. I do not believe everything that he told me, as he had a gift for stories, the details of which sometimes changed with each telling. He claimed to have been all over the country, from Peshawar to Karachi, and indeed even to have crossed into India once, by accident, after he had fallen asleep on the roof of a train, and travelled halfway round the country before he found his way back. He said he had woken one morning to see the Taj Mahal glistening white in the sun, though he claimed to have had no idea which city it was in. 'I couldn't read the station signs,' he said.

Yet some of Karim's stories seemed more authentic than others, and gradually I pieced together the truths of his life. He was an orphan, come from one of the refugee camps; his parents had been Afghanis. In Peshawar he had been a scavenger on rubbish dumps, searching for scraps of paper and plastic, goods that could be sold to recyclers for a few rupees. He had, in the end, learned to read and write a little, having attended a school in the city, run by an English church. But he was dismissive of his education: 'All those classes? What a waste of time! The money was much better on the rubbish dump. I could earn three hundred rupees a day there.'

He had been arrested for pickpocketing—for belonging to a gang of thieves on the Peshawar streets.

'You are a thief, then? I will have to watch myself with you.'

He gave me a disgusted look. 'I am not in here because I stole anything.'

'So, what then?'

'Ah, I am just here because I did not give the police their cut. They were so greedy, man.'

In the hottest days, while I dreamed of waterfalls, he talked incessantly of food, until one of the other prisoners, growing painfully hungry, would shout at him, begging him to shut up.

'I miss the ice cream,' he said. 'There is a shop near Qissa Khawani. You cannot imagine it. It makes my stomach ache just thinking about it.'

'I have eaten ice cream. There was a trolley sometimes at the market in town.'

'No, no. I have seen the stuff they sell in the country. It is not the real thing. They have so many flavours. Chocolate and mango and lemon. I can taste it on my tongue.' Sometimes he would lick his fingers, and I did not laugh at him for it. He made it sound like the most delicious thing on earth.

And yet it was not his greatest passion, not beside movies. He could not believe I had never seen one.

'But there are so many you must see!'

He would launch into lists of names of films that I could not follow, never mind remember. I am not convinced I actually need to see them, because often he would tell me the entire plot, tales of heroes and trusty sidekicks overcoming villains and rescuing their loves. I do not know how he remembered it all. The stories were sometimes so outlandish that I wondered if he were making them up on the spot. He would name the actors for me, tell me what they were famous for, do impressions of their voices. He would tell me that this one was a better singer, while another was a better dancer.

'And which do you prefer?'

'I like them both. But . . .' and he would leap to the name of another actress, '. . . now we're talking. I saw her on the street one day—no word of a lie—and I went and told her that I was a fan and that it would be an honour to be her guide.'

'And did she accept?'

'Of course she accepted! I spent the whole day with her.'

I confessed, once again, that I did not know who she was.

'Ay,' he said, 'you have not even heard of her? What a country boy! You must be the only person in Pakistan. My stories are wasted on you!'

Yet he told them to me anyway. It is true I did not know the people he talked about, but he liked an audience, and in that cell I was the best he would find, the one who tired slowest of his improbable tales and constant chatter.

The prison affected him not at all. Perhaps he had been through worse. Perhaps some people are simply more resistant to the world than I. His spirit was undiminished, as strong the day he left as it had been when he arrived.

As he went he waved to me, saluted the other men. 'See you later boss, I'm out of here.' And he was gone from my life as quickly as he arrived.

I dreamed, once, that I was in a city, walking down a street with you, free in the evening sun. We seemed to know the place, to be at home there. Everything was peaceful and calm. I heard Karim's voice calling to me, and we stopped, and turned to wait for him. And I introduced you both, and he began to tell you stories from the prison, stories he invented, and you looked utterly confused by him, unsure whether to believe him or not. The dream was so clear. I remember precisely the happiness I felt. Even now I can still feel the warmth of it, as though it were something I experienced. Perhaps one day I will come to choose that it was true, so that it will become a memory, and I will forget that it was just a dream.

*

The prison changed, in later years. After they bombed America, and the war came, spilling over the mountains from Afghanistan. I wonder how far it will spread. There has always been violence here, but it is clear from listening to Abbas that it has worsened. I did not fully understand it, but the evidence was there for me. The prison became more crowded than it had ever been. It swelled with men of many nationalities. They came from Saudi Arabia, from Yemen. Some of them bewildered, lost, a long way from their homes. There were months when new men came every day, though many did not stay long.

Some were sold to the Americans as terrorists or insurgents. I am not sure any of them actually were. Some, perhaps, were soldiers, but many of those fought only because they were fed. And innocent men, too—or at least, men guilty of other crimes than fighting Americans—were among those taken. The Americans offered reward money for them, and did not seem to care who they were.

It would have been incomprehensible to me once, but perhaps it is not so hard to understand. Men sold their compatriots because of greed, or because it was a convenient way to dispose of political enemies, or those against whom they wished to revenge themselves. They sold them because the opportunity was there, and perhaps too because it meant they could fool the Americans, could take their money from them, as though this gave them some power over men who exercised so much of it in a country that was not their own.

I saw an American in the prison one day, or think that I did. It is possible I have imagined it, that I conjured the man in my dreams, from the stories that circulated among the prisoners. But I have the memory of a white man standing in the open doorway, dressed in khaki, and wearing sunglasses despite the shade of the cell. Beside him was a Pakistani man in a suit, and the two of them talked as they watched us. The American read names from a list, a short recitation, and the Pakistani man shook his head at each one.

It occurred to me that I might have been among those sold. It would not have been difficult to invent a story: I had been caught crossing the border; I was Afghani, Taliban, an insurgent. I was no longer too young for this to be plausible, and what would my denials matter? I can think only that I was spared because I was too weak. My scarred skin, the slightness of my limbs, spoke of someone who had been imprisoned for years. I still marvel at how thin my legs are; it is a miracle that they support me. No, even the Americans would not have believed I had fought, so I must have been worthless to my jailers.

I had been put in prison not to be punished, but to be forgotten. There had been no trial, no judgement, and perhaps there are no records. Ten years after I entered the prison, even the guards were new, and I knew no one from the time of my arrival there.

ABBAS

When I wake this afternoon the home is quiet. I had been exhausted, as always, by the morning walk, and had slept through the worst of the heat. I am thirsty when I wake, and when I stand my head is flushed and dizzy. I go to fetch some water from the jar in the kitchen, and still can hear nothing. It is late; I have slept for longer than I intended, and I am sure that Alifa has returned from school.

The door to the study is open—Abbas keeps it shut while he works—and there is no sound of anyone within. I tap on the door, and, hearing no reply, look quickly inside for him. Sometimes he is absorbed in a book or paper and does not hear a knock. But he is not there. Before I turn to go, I register a blank space of wall, between two bookshelves, where a painting usually hangs. It is a small work, framed in wood, and held behind glass. A miniature, Abbas calls it. I know nothing of such things, but it seems very beautiful to me, and I have admired it before. In it a woman stands, one hand reaching up into a bush bearing fruit. With her other hand she has cast something to the ground—I cannot see what it is, perhaps a stone or seed or core. Her veil is a clear red, its edges lined with gold paint. Her sideways eye is green. The colours and the detail are wonderful. Each leaf of the bush has its own colour and shape.

I find them in the garden. They sit at the table on the terrace, the miniature laid flat in front of them. They have paper, and a set of paints, and Alifa is attempting to copy the picture.

'Here you are.'

'Yes, with the artist. Would you like to paint?' he asks me. I am tempted, though I feel too old for such things. Abbas sometimes treats me as a child. Perhaps it is not unreasonable. Once, Alifa would have protested, but now her objection is only an act. She rolls her eyes as she does so, but still: she pushes a piece of paper in my direction.

'I suppose he can have a go, too.'

It is hard to suppress a smile. These are small successes, but they bring me tremendous happiness. They have been worth the wait.

'Thank you. But I will just watch, if I am allowed.'

It is clear that the lines of her version of the painting are imperfect, that the image of the woman is looser, bent slightly out of shape. But she has an eye for the work. Tiny details from the original appear on her paper without prompting from her father.

'Slower, Alifa. There is no need to show off for our guest. Look at how her hand is turned, like this. Is this how yours is?'

She studies the miniature and makes the gesture with her own hand, and then corrects her painting.

'There, you see it. Excellent.'

She shoots me a glance that is partly pride, and partly a plain message that she does not think I could do anywhere near as well. I have no doubt of it, and I bow my head to acknowledge her mastery, but she has already returned to her painting. She has such fierce concentration, while my

own mind tends to wander. Even if I once owned such discipline, it is long gone.

It is such a pleasure to see father and daughter together.
I will miss them terribly when I leave. As I sit and watch
them I think of my sisters, sitting perhaps at some distant
table with my father. Though of course my sisters are
grown, and it is an idle, futile daydream.

I fetch my notebook and sit a little way apart from them
to write for a while, and then put it aside to go to make
bread in the tandoor. These are such ordinary actions,
requiring no great effort, but the novelty, the rarity, has not
yet worn away. I hope you will understand why I tell you
the details of such minor things, and can feel something of
the pleasure I find in them.

The Prison

They did not tell me why I was released. It was miraculous, I suppose, though I was numb to the miracle of it. One day a guard said my name, and came to unchain me, and I went with him obediently. I did not know if I was to be moved to a different cell, or being taken to be beaten. He led me out through tiled corridors, unlocking gates as we passed, and pushed me out through a door. We went through the yard, and I instinctively craned my neck upwards, searching the sky for the swallows. I stumbled as I did so, and the guard muttered in frustration, dragging me on through the entrance of the prison, the gates opening to let us pass. He left me standing at the roadside. I did not trust him. It was a strange trick he was playing. I stood there for a long time, waiting for them to bring me back inside. When my legs felt weak I sat down in the dust, and then the gates opened once more and the guard returned, but it was only to shout at me, and to kick and curse me until I moved away.

I was disorientated and exhausted. I did not know where I was, or what I should do. The wide openness of the land was terrifying. My chest filled with panic, and I almost returned to the prison gates, to be let back in. Only the fear of violence restrained me. I suppose I walked away. After that, I do not remember much.

I must have walked for a long time. I think that I must have stopped a passing lorry driver for help, because I have a fragment of memory in which I am sitting in a cabin which vibrates wildly over the engine beneath. I remember the diesel fumes, and being thrown about by rough roads; I remember clutching my arms around my stomach, pressing the points of my fingers hard into my breastbone, to keep myself from being sick.

I do not know how I began to find my way. I did not reach my family, who in any case were no longer there, but I came close to my old home, fell only a few miles short. I am not even sure I was walking in the right direction when I collapsed into a ditch, in which place I was found, some time later, by Abbas, as he walked with his friends to the tea shop for an evening of conversation over games of backgammon.

I was in prison for fifteen years. I am twenty-nine years old. My body belongs to a much older man. It is a relic I know too intimately: these scars, this broken form.

All those years! They took everything from me. My health and my family. They took from me the person I might have been, and returned in its place half a man, a shadow. Even now I am not sure I will feel lasting pleasure again. My capacity for it has been damaged. The suffering has retreated, but it leaves behind it an absence, a joylessness. If you are able, imagine breathing, and nothing stirring within. Yes, I feel relief that I am free, and it is a deep relief at that, but there is no joy. My pleasures have gone from me, like petals pulled from a flower head, or lost to a winter frost.

And yet something has emerged intact from those years. A second miracle, perhaps. I still long for you. I still feel love for you. I do not know how the feeling was not destroyed. You may want me to say that it is because love is strong, but the darkness I have told you of was stronger still: it could erase the universe, wipe clean the stars from the night sky. I did not think love could stand against such power and I wonder and marvel that it has been spared.

This is what they did to me, my love. What was it they did to you? I beg you to tell me, because I have been helpless to know.

The Orchard

The walk comes a little easier today. The pain in my legs lessens as I go, and I am able to lengthen my stride. I know I must try to improve my posture. I walk half bent over, and my joints protest and my back aches when I try to straighten. It is partly physical, the consequence of ill-treatment and of living for years in cramped spaces. I am still not used to having the freedom to stretch. But it is also habit, my body naturally forming a defensive shape, curled around itself, still waiting to be beaten.

Through the trees, out of sight from where I sit, is our neighbour's house—how strange that I still think of them as my neighbours—where once, long ago, a wedding was held. I have always thought that I would one day walk down to it, to see if it remained as before, but so far I have not felt the need. I knew as soon as I reached the orchard that this was the right place. Here, where the low wall ends, with my back against the tree.

Today I am sitting and watching the ants. Their highway runs not far from my feet, the insects pouring in both directions along it. I have brought a handful of almonds to eat and I cup them in both hands, raising them to my face to breathe the faint smell of them. It rouses a hunger in me, though a very pleasant one, because it brings an anticipation I know is easily sated. I eat them one at a time, until I reach the last, and this I break into smaller pieces, placing them in a small pile not far from the ant trail. They are quick to locate them: one of the creatures deviates its course until it has found them, and in its path follow several others, until a sinuous ribbon of insects flows between trail and almond. The first ant seems to make a failed attempt at nudging a small piece of nut along, perhaps weighing it up, but then miraculously lifts it and with no loss of speed returns to the main channel of ants. The rest of the pile is similarly tackled by a small swarm, the pieces ferried on their backs, sometimes hoisted up with another ant still clinging to it, so that the worker carries both nut and ant. Soon the food has disappeared and the new ribbon gradually twirls and thins until it is absorbed back into the main channel. Only one or two stray ants still criss-cross the area, searching for any fragments that have been missed.

The ants do not scatter when I stand, though I am careful not to step on them. Go into your dwellings, ants, lest Solomon and his warriors should unwittingly crush you!

Among the branches the pomegranates are ripening. The last of the petals from their flowers has fallen. I was tempted to take one, but they are not yet at their best, the colour of their skin not yet warm, and so I will be patient. The promise of a fruit freshly opened, its juice running from broken arils, is exquisite, and will enable the walk to come easier still. I have longed to taste one again. The thought of it is enough to cause my mouth to water, my stomach to gurgle. The memory of that taste is no less than the memory of my childhood. Whenever my sisters or I suffered an upset stomach we were given a cup of juice, morning and evening while we were ill, to settle our bellies once again. We were given pomegranate to soothe cuts and grazes, to ease coughs, to cool fever.

What an extraordinary thing is memory. Those endless days in the prison, their empty routines still imprinted into the lines of my skin, fade from me. Already they are becoming like a story once told to me, and then remembered, as though at a remove. They are clouded with doubt, and of the suffering which was so certain, it is hard now to say what was truth, and what nightmare.

And yet, sitting here, if I close my eyes and reach my arms into the low limbs of the tree, in an instant I am a child again, riding on my father's back, marvelling at the world high in the branches, the bright sunlight filtering through.

I Am Afraid

I am afraid, Saba, that you have long forgotten me. No, more than this. I have thought about it so much, and I will not hide my thoughts from you. I am afraid that if I am remembered, even fondly, then the strength of my feeling will disturb you. That when we meet you will be saddened to see that I have remained a child, while you have freed yourself from those adolescent emotions, and have become a woman.

Will you read this and think that it has become an obsession for me? This feeling, which once was real, but that has come to exist only in my own heart? Love must be shared, or else it is just madness. Have I, like Ibraheem Jamal, with his thoughts of revenge, allowed my ideas to separate from the world, so that they became something larger and more powerful, so that I must always live in them, and never again with the truth? The idea of you was strong enough to twist the world, to do strange things to my mind. I am afraid that by clinging on to that idea, I changed the truth of what we had beyond repair. That by taking it into the darkness I allowed it to corrupt, that it became something wholly of my imagination.

Such are my fears. And it is true that I was overcome with panic when I thought of you, when I did not know where you were, or what you might be doing. That I was almost sick with jealousy of those who were able to know you. I knew it was futile, I knew it was senseless, but I could not help myself. I thought of you constantly, obsessively. I had to endure the impossible frustration of not knowing, and the knowledge that you knew nothing of me, that in an instant I had ceased to be a part of your life. I wanted so much for you just to know that I was alive.

But listen to me: I did not arbitrarily choose you. I clung on to you because it was of you that my heart was most sure. With you I had no doubts; with you I always knew.

I have said that I do not know the boy I once was. In truth, all that remains of him is this love for you. It was the only thing that survived. It was the strongest thing I had, which was why I held on to it so firmly. Even as it condemned me to terrible unhappiness I was saved by it. Or if no longer by love, then by the memory of love, which is as strong.

If I ask my heart now, *do I love you?* then the answer leaps swiftly back, overwhelming and certain: *yes.* I feel it with every part of me. And I trust my heart, because I have nothing else. But the truth is that it has been a long time, and even I, now, doubt my feelings. Is it possible to love someone for so long, in their absence, and for that love to remain unbroken and true? We have been apart for so long. Over the years, in my mind, you must have become something you are not; a construction that bears little resemblance to the person you really are. I struggle to be sure even who *I* once was, before all this. How, then, can I know you, without knowing anything about your life?

It is impossible to resolve these things alone. I have thought that all I need to do is to see you, and then I will know. Then everything, the doubt and confusion, will clear, and all that is merely an illusion will fade away. And so I hope for this. But I am afraid, too, because I no longer trust that the answers life gives us are so simple, or so sure.

The Orchard

Today I broke open a pomegranate. I have been watching them carefully, and the earliest among them are beautifully ripe. I knew I should not take one, but I could not resist. Its absence will hardly be noticed, and my body has been so thirsty for the taste. *Eat of their fruits when they ripen*, says the Qur'an. I spent a long time choosing the finest one I could find, whose skin was firm, glowing like your cheeks in the morning light. I picked it carefully, so as not to disturb the other fruits around it, and then I held its weight in my hand, gripping it with my palm and fingers, skin against skin. To test its ripeness I held it to my ear and tapped it, and was rewarded with that strange and perfect sound, almost metallic in its tone.

I dug my thumbs together to break the outer rind, and then prised the fruit apart, opening it into two halves, watching the inner cells tear away from the soft, bitter tissue that holds them. My hands shook as I raised it to my mouth. And the taste of the juice on my tongue! It was so sweet my lips quivered, but with that faint dry sourness in my mouth afterwards. It was wonderful. I gulped down the pieces, careful not to miss a single aril. When we were young, my mother told us this hadith: that the pomegranate was among the trees grown in the gardens of paradise, and that all such trees are descended from it. So, within each fruit is a pip that belongs to that original tree, and when we eat, we must not miss a single aril, in case it is the sacred one. This I did as a child, and this, from a habit that is still pleasing to me, I do again now.

When I had finished the fruit I felt instantly greedy for a second, and I stood to reach for more. I was overcome by a sudden swell of indignation, a sense that the orchard, after all, once belonged to my family, that it should not have been taken from us. But the feeling passed as quickly as it had come, and I stood there with my arms reaching upwards, feeling foolish, and I did not pick anything, but walked home instead, the pleasure in my heart gone, and the sweetness in my mouth turned sour.

My Father

I learned yesterday that my father is dead. Beloved, I feel such pain in my chest. All those years when I had hoped to see him. All those years when I did not know what had become of my family, nor they me. Oh my father. My heart tears, and then becomes solid again, a crack across its centre that will not heal.

The news came from Abbas, who has continued making enquiries on my behalf. He told me gently. He had spoken to a man who knew the orchard, and remembered when it belonged to my family. The man's story was unclear in parts—he was unsure if my father's illness had meant the orchard needed to be given up, or if it was taken from them, handed over to a local tribal elder, in exchange for loyalty or favours done. But whatever the truth of the matter, my father had indeed been ill, and had died soon after the orchard was gone. His family had moved south, to Multan, he thought.

And all this ten years ago. Ten years of not knowing—it is hard to bear. I wonder what the illness was, and when it fell. It is all too easy to imagine the loss of the orchard being too much for my father, causing his heart to break. A terrible fear returns to me of old, that I was the cause of everything, of every disaster; that I brought not just shame on myself, but ruin to my family.

There was some meagre hope in the news. The mention of Multan—cousins of my mother live there, and it does not seem unlikely that, having had to leave, she may have gone to them. I do not have an address, but I remember the family name, and at last I have somewhere to begin. Still, in the circumstances, I am afraid that I would not be welcome, that they would not want me. Perhaps it is better that I am believed dead, and can bring down no more troubles upon them.

I slept poorly last night, and was plagued by anxious dreams. I am torn by grief and shame. My stomach feels sick and my insides rotten, as though all the months of recovery have been for nothing.

I have felt little better today, and the morning walk brought me no pleasure. I am weary from it, but still cannot sleep, and so I am staying late in the garden tonight, allowing the temperature of the air to fall and the stars to brighten against the dark. I shiver and shake from the cold. It is refreshing after the dusty heat on the road this morning, and I am trying to allow myself to feel cleansed by it.

Some summer nights when I was a child, we would sleep outside. My father would carry carpets from the house and lay them in piles on the roof, and then unroll our mattresses over them. We would lie on the mounds, wrapping ourselves in blankets. After the heat of the day the cold would be blissful, and I could burrow down beneath the weight of my covers. My mother would tell stories of the stars until we fell asleep. I wish I remembered all the stories. I can still find the two stars I know were sisters in some tale, and that one had followed a prince to a faraway land, and remained there, even after the prince had died, separated from her twin by the great misty stream of stars that ran between them.

So I sit outside, watching for the blazing trails of shooting stars, marvelling at the vastness of creation. It is amazing how all these are the same stars we used to see, their numbers uncountable, the sky so thick with them that they blur together. I try to push down the guilt. But our actions cannot be undone. It is another weight I will have to live with. It feels heavy tonight, and the cold will not take it from me.

The Village

When I was young I had no sense of change. I did not know that ways of life could simply pass, or that entire peoples could be forced from their homes, that villages could cease to be. Time stretches out in our youth, and everything is simply as it is. Our parents and grandparents are always present, and do not seem to age. A home is a fixed, unchanging thing that can always be returned to, and children remain children, their pleasures and needs simple and constant. The world is what it is.

But now change comes so fast. The war, which has skirted these valleys without entering them, begins to threaten. The borders are crossed by armies, as well as by ideas. There are new voices being raised, whose words reach even me, quiet within the walls of Abbas's garden. They demand the imposition of Sharia. When they speak of *tradition*, they do not mean the way of life we have known for generations. The fortune-tellers will be beaten from the market, the schools closed. They do not speak of us as belonging to Pakistan any more. Perhaps that land has always been a distant, imaginary nation, one that belonged to the plains, whose reach did not extend to these high areas.

Last week a bomb was thrown over the wall of a girls' school in the neighbouring valley. Two children and a teacher were killed by splintering metal. It is hard to believe that it is happening here, among the places of my childhood. The men who did this are strangers to me; they have read a different book from the one I studied, years ago. But I think that I understand them. I have seen how anger spills out when it is kept from striking that which imprisons it. It needs to fall somewhere, and so it falls on those who are unable to defend themselves. Such men act to feel powerful, to assert their world upon us. They believe that they must prevail, or else all is lost. And they are not afraid to destroy, because they do not understand what it is they are destroying.

'It is because they themselves were not educated,' I say. 'They are afraid of it, of what people might learn.'

Abbas sighs, and recites: 'Learning makes a good man better, but an ill man worse.' He looks at me. 'It is a proverb,' he explains. 'Both sad and true.'

Alifa's own school has been closed since then, though Abbas is hopeful that it will reopen. He is away from the house often, talking with his friends and the village leaders, agitating for calm, for reason.

Still, he is unhappy that I continue with my morning walks.

'But what would such men want with me?' I ask. 'I have no money, nothing for them to take.'

'They are looking for recruits.'

'But I do not wish to join them.'

He looks at me to see if I am serious. Sometimes he forgets that I know little of the world.

'I do not think that would be a popular position with them,' he says.

He has made me careful, at least. As I walk I stop from

time to time, no longer to gather my breath, but instead to watch ahead and behind for movement. I have not encountered anyone, save for the occasional goatherd, wandering with his animals through the high ground, or the passing of a lone truck, cheerfully painted and bejewelled as though for a wedding. One morning a man came towards me on a motorcycle, a simple, ancient machine, little more than a bicycle with a small engine attached. Three large boxes were stacked precariously behind him, held by rope. I stepped to the side of the road, but he did not even look at me, keeping his eyes firmly fixed on the uneven road as the cycle putt-putted forwards, carrying him along at little more than walking pace. I do not know where he had come from, or where he was heading. So for now, at least, my walks continue. If the roads become unsafe for me, then how much more will they be for you, and then the purpose of my journeys will in any case fail.

In the orchard the pomegranates hang ripely on the trees, their red skins darkening by the day, turning to crimsons and purples. They should have been picked by now. Every morning I arrive expecting the branches to be emptied, but still they are full. It is clear that the owner is neglectful of his crop. Perhaps it is simply that he does not know what he is doing, or perhaps he does not need the income, and the orchard was indeed merely a gift he did not want, a payment for some service rendered or some loyalty proven. It would make me terribly sad to think so, to see land that was tended for years with love given over to greed and waste. The fruit will begin to split if it is left for much longer. Soon, the touch of rain on its stretched skin will be enough to cause it to swell and open. A storm will devastate the crop.

The Garden

Today I sit with Alifa while she reads from her books. She has been missing school, and we have been fasting, too, which does not greatly improve her mood in the afternoons. But she has decided to expend her frustrated scholarly energies on me, and so we have ended up spending more time on my own reading and writing than on hers. Alifa is a far stricter teacher than her father. Abbas kindly allows me to make my own mistakes, and if in my own time I do not see them he will gently draw my attention towards them. But his daughter watches my pen intently, and pounces the instant the inevitable mistake is made, taking the pen from my hand and correcting it, then pointing, exasperated, at the new version on the page.

'Ah yes,' I say. 'You are quite right. How clumsy of me.'

She gives a brief nod of satisfaction and we continue, until the next mistake.

Her stamina for this type of work is greater than mine, and my attention wanders long before hers has begun to. She persists with me for a while, until, perhaps deciding I am a hopeless case, she leans back from the book.

'You won't get any better if you don't try.'

I nod, faking a melancholy I do not feel. 'It is such a shame,' I say, 'because you are a good teacher.'

She wrinkles her nose in thought for a moment, as though to decide whether I am teasing her.

'I think so too,' she says, and she sounds so sure of it, so serious, that I cannot help but laugh. She starts at the sound—I doubt she has heard me laugh once in the months I have been here—and then looks hurt, and I have to be swift to mollify her.

The truth is, I am simply grateful for her help. I have had so much to say to you, and had wondered for a long time how I might do so. In person, it would come in a rush. I would have too much to tell, and no way to begin. This way, I have not needed to tell you everything at once, but just one piece at a time, measured out in bites, as though you were eating a fruit. And if you do come to read these words, then you can be sure that the passages have been immeasurably smoothed, their mistakes excised, thanks to the close attentions of a child who is a significantly better writer than I will ever be.

THE ORCHARD

Good morning, trees; good morning, wall. Hello, my ant friends. I do not know how many more days I will be able to come and meet you here.

They are harvesting the fruit at last, though they are doing so carelessly. There are pomegranates broken underfoot. They were so ripe they might have split open as soon as they were touched, and then have been cast aside as worthless. For those that did not, it is still too late. If it is picked early, the fruit will store for months, its sweetness safe within the tough rind. But it has been left too long, and now the fruit will continue to ripen after it has been taken from the trees, so that much of it will be spoiled by the time it has reached the market stands. Perhaps the owners know this, perhaps they are ignorant. Perhaps they do not care.

I wonder if I, too, have come too late. If you came here once before and satisfied your curiosity. If you came many years ago, and allowed yourself to put the past from your mind, and will never come again. It is possible, but I have come, all the same. I have always hoped.

There are times when I think I would suffer all those years again, if you would only come.

Soon I will have to leave. Abbas thinks it is time. I am not sure he will ever ask me to go, but he makes it clear that he fears for my safety. He has offered, indirectly, to purchase a bus ticket to Multan for me, and has hinted that if I need to go further than that he will be able to help again, that he has friends who will find papers for me.

And I know he is right. Though I have not exhausted my friend's hospitality—surely, I must have tested its limits—I have stayed far longer than I expected to, and far longer than I was entitled to. For one thing, I am no longer too sick to move on. The walk was easier this morning; my body hurt less and the air came smoothly to my lungs. I am not whole—I do not think I will ever be that again—but I am well. More than I believed was possible.

I have been selfish, these last months. But it has been so pleasant to stay! I have had here the comfort and the company I had lacked for so long, and I have drawn out the days as much as I have been able to. Simply, I am afraid of the future, afraid of uncertainty. In the prison my days were meted out for me. I am unaccustomed to having choices, which seem to spread wider and wider, like many paths overlapping and opening into plains of fear. How much better it would be to stay here, to spend my mornings in the orchard, my days in the garden.

Yet I know in my heart that I cannot. I must travel south, away from the mountains. I have to find my family, and I will have to find work. To rouse my courage I imagine Multan, summoning an image of the city waiting for me as though it were the one that Karim used to talk of, full of wonder and life, with cinemas, and ice-cream sellers running stalls at the roadside. I picture film stars walking the streets, a cheerful pickpocket dancing along at their heels.

But I cannot leave yet. Not yet. Who knows where I will

be next year—if I will be able to return? I count the days remaining for me at the orchard, one at a time. *Insha'Allah* I will come tomorrow, and then I will come the next day. After that, I do not know. All things are possible.

THE GARDEN

The rains came yesterday, in the afternoon. All morning long the air felt heavy, and the breeze came sluggish and too warm from the south. The sky was a single cloud without any colour to it, almost invisible until it began to blacken. After I had returned from the orchard I stood at the gate with Alifa, watching the lightning in the distance, listening to thunder which came dimly at first, but grew in power as it tumbled up the valley, and came finally to sound like the crack of an enormous whip or a switch in the air above us. We both jumped at the sound of it, and Alifa gave a stifled squeak of fear before retreating inside. It was an immense sound that seemed to completely fill the vast spaces of the sky. The valley darkened beneath the clouds and though the sight was beautiful I felt very small and powerless in the world. I was not far behind Alifa in returning inside.

This morning I tried to reach the orchard again, but the downpour had been heavy on the mountain, and a torrent had swept away the road. I stood at the edge of the landslide, thinking to pick my way across it, but the slough was thick and muddy and still slowly flowed over the side of the road. I did not trust that I had the strength to cross it without getting stuck, and so I turned around and came back to sit in the garden.

The storm will have destroyed the last of the fruit in the orchard. It is winter now; the season is over. If we are fortunate we might perhaps have a few last days of good weather after the storm is done, but nothing is certain.

Abbas worked the morning in his study and came to sit with me as I finished preparing lunch. I tried again, as I had many months earlier, to show him how grateful I was. 'I want to thank you for your hospitality. I will never forget it.'

He smiled, and tilted his head to one side in recognition.

We shook hands.

'Alifa will miss you,' he said. 'Not that she will say so.'

'She will find other poor students to bully. And no doubt they will be more attentive than I have been.'

He nodded, amused, though the smile fell quickly, and his face was downcast.

'Things will not be easy for her,' he said.

'But you'll stay?'

'As Allah wills it.'

I try to understand his generosity. I have imagined myself in his position, owning a home, and taking in a sick man I had found in the street. Providing him with a bed, clothes and food, paying for his medication. And each time I fail. I am ashamed by it, but the truth is that I cannot see myself acting as he has acted. Perhaps it is the instinct of self-protection, learned from the prison, or perhaps only a childish selfishness I have not yet had the chance to outgrow. Either way, I must try to be like this man, as much as I am able. I must study him as I have studied his books, and I must try to learn the lessons.

After we had eaten I helped Abbas tidy the garden,

sweeping the paths while he cleared debris from the flower beds. And then I stayed a while to write there until the rain returned and drove me inside once more. The storm tonight has not been so violent as yesterday's, but the drops are fat and thick in the air, and slap heavily on the floor as they land.

Tomorrow, then, if the weather relents, and if the road is passable. One last day.

The Orchard

Saba, beloved, forgive me if you are tiring of this story. I have just one part of it left to tell. A part that is not my own, but which is about a friend I once knew. I knew her for only the shortest of times, many years ago. Perhaps you will object that I have been gone too long, that I could know nothing of her now. Well, it is true, I know almost nothing. She is a stranger, no longer the girl she once was, and she has lived a life that has taken her far from me. I know neither what she has encountered nor how it may have changed her, know nothing about the circumstances of her life.

All things are possible. If the shame of what is said to have happened to her long ago did not ruin her, then she may live far from here, she may be married and have children who are as bright-eyed and quick-witted as their mother. She may love her husband, she may be happy. I have hoped only for her happiness. You must not imagine that I would wish to take it from her. I know that she will not, cannot possibly, have held on to the thought of me in the same way I have held on to that of her.

But I believe that she still remembers this place, that she thinks of it more often than she allows herself to admit. She remembers how beautiful the trees are in the early morning, how swift the birds that dart between them. And she remembers with something close to sadness the boy she once knew there, even though she does not know what became of him, even though she may suppose he is dead.

I believe, too, that there will be days when the ache of memory needs to be soothed inside her, when it will wake her early, before the dawn speaks into her room. From time to time—perhaps when the pomegranates are in season and appearing in the market—the ache will come so powerfully that she will rise and dress, and in the near-dark will make her way from the house, muttering, if she needs to, excuses of work to be done or relatives to be visited.

If it is not a long way, she will travel to the town she grew up in, and to the valley above it. In the rose dawn light she will climb the road, the mountains glorious in their paleness. They will surround her and protect her; their familiar weight will be a comfort at her side. On the mountain air she will smell traces of wild jasmine.

She will walk until she comes to places she once knew well, and when she has reached them she will make her way finally to an old orchard, where the last of the season's fruit clings, rotten, to the trees. The rest has been picked, though late, too late. As the sun's light begins to step down from its lofty peaks she will find her way to a particular tree, against the roots of which she once slept. And there she will pause, the solitude of her morning walk broken. Beneath the tree a man will be sitting, in the exact place she herself had planned to sit.

She will be cautious of him, perhaps a little afraid, but the man will not rise, nor reproach her for being there alone. He will seem not to notice her at all, though his position affords him an excellent view over the path, and he must have seen her approaching from a long way back. He will sit with his shawl wrapped around him, his head bent over the notebook he has brought with him, a pen swimming swiftly among its last pages.

She will watch him for a minute, until something in his nature or aspect decides for her that he is harmless—perhaps she will notice how the swallows are undisturbed by his presence. Her confidence will return, and she will bow her head and greet him, *As-salaam alaykum*, intending to ask perhaps about the orchard, about the family it once belonged to. For a long moment he will not reply, as though he has not heard. The air will be still. His pen will continue to slide along the paper. Eventually, it will stop, with the assurance of a story finally closed, and his hands will rest. He will raise his face to her, and she will see above his beard a familiar angle to his cheeks, take in the precise colour of his eyes. In a sudden second she will know him, and the words she was preparing will slip from her mind.

For a moment, you will each wonder if what you are seeing is real. And then he will look you in the eyes and smile. He will greet you as though you had been apart only a day.

'My swallow,' he will say. 'I was just waiting for you.'

His hands will wrap a long string around his notebook to bind it. He will stand, and carefully, like a child offering a piece of fruit, he will hold out the book to you.

'Here,' he will say. 'Take this. It is for you. It is finished.'

ABOUT THE AUTHOR

Peter Hobbs grew up in Cornwall and Yorkshire, England. His debut novel, *The Short Day Dying*, was published by Faber in 2005. It won a Betty Trask Award and was shortlisted for the Whitbread First Novel Award, the John Llewellyn Rhys Prize, and the 2007 International IMPAC Dublin Literary Award. A collection of stories, *I Could Ride All Day in My Cool Blue Train*, was published in 2006.